Smudge

by

J.D. Webb

Smudge

Cover Art by *Debbie Taylor*

The Wild Rose Press, Inc.
PO Box 708
Adams Basin, NY 14410-0708
Visit us at www.thewildrosepress.com

Publishing History
First Crimson Rose Mainstream Mystery Edition, 2014
Print ISBN 978-1-62830-306-3
Digital ISBN 978-1-62830-307-0

Published in the United States of America

"Jim, something happened at the ATM. I'm kinda shook up."

"What was that?" He leaned against the doorway, gnawing on a piece of provolone.

"I found an injured woman next to the bank. She'd been beaten and left for dead."

"Good Lord! I guess that's why you're so wet." Jim's expression didn't change. He ran a finger along her cheek and she shivered. "Well, it's all over now, sweetie. Let's have something to eat. Come on. It'll do you good to busy yourself in the kitchen." He took her arm and tried to lead her down the hall.

Maybe it was the trauma she'd been through or the weariness of being mindful of how Jim would react, but Trish surprised herself by snatching her arm away. Beads of water sprayed the hallway. "You aren't listening. I don't want to cook. I've had a traumatic experience. I'm cold and wet. I'm going up to shower and then go to bed."

Jim stood silently, his arm frozen in the position it had been in when she jerked away. His eyes narrowed and his smile disappeared. "I guess I can find something myself. But, dear, don't ever pull away from me like that again." Slowly his 6-foot-3 frame headed to the kitchen.

Trish breathed a sigh of relief and hung her sopping coat on the back of Jim's prized Louis the Fourteenth desk chair. *Screw the chair*. Her heart fluttered and she knew her blood pressure was elevated from the events of the evening and then the confrontation. Her breath caught in her chest when she spotted some dark brown splotches on her fuchsia leather coat.

Praise for *SMUDGE*

"Trisha Morgan is a great character, believable, strong, yet vulnerable, and her buddy Heather is a hoot. The reader is rooting for them both in this fast-paced story."

~Barbara D'Amato

~*~

"Hold on to your hat, because Webb has done it again with a tale that keeps the reader turning the pages. Don't forget to make sure the windows and doors are locked. To tell you any more would give away the twists and turns in the plot...and we wouldn't want to do that, would we?"

~Morgan St. James

Dedication

To Judi, my best friend, first editor, and soul mate.
Thanks for over 45 years of fun and bliss.

Chapter One

Tonight of all nights, why is the traffic so heavy?
How can there be a traffic jam in a town with only
1,241 residents? Twelve hundred forty-one and a half,
now that Mrs. Purvis has entered her second trimester.
Get out of the way, Mr. Lavery. Pay attention. Seems
like everyone in Millvale, Illinois, and two surrounding
counties wants to be downtown at 8 pm.

Trisha Morgan flashed her lights and pulled around
John Lavery's car, giving him a half-hearted wave. She
continued to the only ATM in town to grab enough
money to cover tomorrow's breakfast with the girls. All
were employees of Spitzer, Walters, Walters, and
Sloan, the premier law firm in town. Okay, the only law
firm in town.

Each Friday morning Trish and her friends Joan,
Charity and Heather met at Jan's Java Hut to rehash the
oddities and inequities of SWW&S. The small
coffeehouse refused to take credit cards, which
necessitated her trip to the cash machine. No reason
other than the weekly date with good friends would get
her to make a side trip to the bank.

Well, isn't that amazing? A parking spot right in
front of the bank.

Trish signaled and eased Jim's car into the space,
cringing at the scrape of the wheel against the curb.
Thankfully, the curb didn't gouge the side of his new

Jaguar. She shivered and tried not to think of the consequences of causing damage to her husband's newest plaything. With her Escort in the shop again, she had been allowed to borrow Jim's car—but only for the day.

Grabbing her umbrella, she cursed as the release button refused to operate. Damn, just long enough for the rain to make her mascara run. Finally, it opened; she splashed through puddles, across the sidewalk to the front of the Citizens' National Bank of Millvale.

As usual, the light over the ATM had not been replaced, so she dug her small flashlight out of her purse and approached the open-sided kiosk. Juggling umbrella and flashlight in one hand, she inserted her card and waited for the machine to activate. She swiped a smudge off the screen with her hand so she could see to enter her PIN.

Ugh! Wet and sticky. Dropping the umbrella, Trish rummaged a tissue from her purse and quickly scrubbed her hand. She shined the light on her palm, revealing a dark red smear.

Oh, my God! It's blood! Her thoughts stalled as the ATM ate her card for the second time in two weeks.

The moan seemed to come from beneath her feet. Trish's head swiveled left and right. Just darkness and rain drenching her good Nike sweats. Traffic trickled past. She cocked her ear, straining to hear any noise. Nothing.

"Hello? Someone there?" Silence. Maybe the sound wasn't what she thought. Trish looked over her shoulder hoping to see someone she could call for help, but the sidewalk was deserted. She wanted to find the source of the groan, and then again, she really didn't.

Someone may be hurt and needs help. She picked up the umbrella and willed her feet to move toward the corner of the bank building, her reservations replaced by concern. Squeezing her flashlight in a death grip, she let the light play out on the sidewalk and into the darkness between buildings.

An alley ran between the bank and the drug store. Trash cans and debris littered the interior as far as she could see in the limited light. Trish listened, hoping the moan had been a figment of her imagination. She took baby steps through the wetness and strewn garbage.

"Help...me."

The barely audible plea came from beyond an overflowing container in front of her. Trish looked behind her once, praying someone familiar would appear. No one came. She wanted to run. Get the police. But she couldn't make herself move.

"Is someone here?"

A whisper came from the side of a huge green dumpster. "Please...help."

Trish crept toward the voice. There. Light from her flashlight shone on a woman lying on her back. Then Trish saw the pool of blood near the woman's head.

"Help."

Trish dug for her cell phone and hit the 911 speed dial.

"Nine one one, emergency."

"Help! Someone is injured in the alley beside the Citizens' National Bank. I need an ambulance here right away." Trish gave her name and answered the rest of the dispatcher's questions quickly. She tucked her cell phone into her jacket pocket and dropped her purse next to the injured woman. Trish slipped off her jacket and then her cardigan.

Draping the sweater over the woman's chest, she wriggled back into her jacket and knelt beside the woman. "Help is coming. Hang in there." Trish leaned the umbrella so that it partially shielded the woman from the steady drizzle. There was so much blood! Where was the ambulance? What had happened?

Blood covered the left side of the woman's face and head. Trish wished she could remember her first-aid training class from several years ago. The huge sad eyes closed as the woman lost consciousness.

Thirty seconds later, the distant wail of a siren drifted through the darkness. The ambulance arrived, followed by a Millvale police car. And, oh gosh, it was Bob Jenkins. Not that he was a bad cop or anything. In high school, they had been a hot item for two years. That had been over fifteen years ago.

With bustling efficiency, the EMTs took over, and Bob, who constituted half of the entire police force, greeted her. He escorted her away from the emergency workers.

They stopped at the ATM. "Okay, Trish, what happened here?"

"I don't know." Her hands shook and she gripped her purse to steady them. Both purse zippers gaped open; she fumbled sliding them shut. "I stopped to use the ATM and heard moaning." She opened her palm to him. "I got blood on my hand." She stole a quick glance back toward the alley. "I went to investigate, then called nine one one."

The EMTs rolled a gurney out of the darkness and toward the ambulance. An IV drip hung from a man's outstretched hand as he pushed the sheet-draped stretcher. Trish looked away. "All that blood. I thought I might be sick for a minute there."

"Let's get you out of the rain. You're soaked and probably cold. My car's just over there." He followed Trish and opened the rear door for her.

Trish thankfully sank into the stale-smelling back seat and shivered.

Bob closed the door. He scanned the entire area and moved to the back of the squad car. He removed a blanket from the trunk, opened the back door once more, and draped the blanket over Trish.

Grateful for the added warmth, she wrapped the coverlet around her as tightly as she could. "Thanks."

He still had that same fabulous smile. "Forgive me for not getting you out of the rain sooner. As far as crime goes, Millvale's normally a pretty quiet town. I guess this kind of spooked me. Wait here for a second."

Bob unrolled a line of yellow and black crime-scene tape and attached it in a semi-circle around the ATM. He stopped once and picked up what appeared to be a credit card off the sidewalk directly in front of the ATM. He took out a plastic bag, dropped the object inside, and stuffed it into his shirt pocket. Then he headed back down the alley.

Trish checked her watch. *Oh no. Jim's going to be royally pissed that I'm so late.* She fished her cell phone from her jacket and called home. She waited for the answering machine message. "Hi, we're not home right now. Leave a message and if we recognize the name, we'll call back." Jim was proud of that message. He felt it conveyed humor and let people know they were a fun couple. *Like that was true.*

"Jim, I got delayed. I'm not sure how long I'll be.

I'm okay, just had some trouble at the ATM. I'll be home soon."

Bob appeared at the corner of the building talking to old Doc Winters. The silver-haired family doctor had brought most of the Millvale residents into the world. He served as the local MD and coroner. They finished and Bob waved after Doc, who shuffled toward his older model sedan.

Bob returned to the squad car and got into the front seat. Leather upon leather creaked and he handed her the umbrella she'd been carrying. She nodded thanks. He picked up a clipboard and began writing.

"Do you think she'll be okay?"

Bob turned and propped a leg on the seat. "Doc says she has a probable concussion. Head wounds always bleed like hell. Do you know her?"

"Never saw her before. At least I don't think I know her. With all the blood and everything, it was hard to tell."

"Her name is Elizabeth Thompson. I found her ATM card in front of the bank."

Trish shook her head. "Nope. The name's not familiar."

"None of us recognized her, either. Well, the chief'll want you to come to the station tomorrow and give a statement."

"I guess I could stop by on my lunch hour. About noon okay?"

"Fine." Bob paused and shifted his position. "Trish, think back. Did you see anything unusual when you pulled up—anyone lurking around or maybe a car shooting away?"

"Nothing at all. There seemed to be a lot of traffic

for this time of night and in the middle of the week. Nothing else out of the ordinary. Didn't notice any unfamiliar cars." Trish laid the blanket on the seat. "Is that all? I really ought to get home."

Bob nodded. "That's it for now."

She got out of the car, flicked the button on her umbrella, and it popped open.

Jenkins exited and touched his cap. "Till noon tomorrow. Nice to see you, Trish. You still look great." Without waiting for a response, he turned and hurried back to the crime scene.

Trish stood frozen in her tracks. *How could he say that? I must look like a drowned rat.* As if to provide evidence, a rivulet of rain rushed down her face. It tasted of hair spray.

She had to admit Bob looked great, too. His hair still black and wavy. No hint of gray and, just like in high school, a few uncooperative locks spilling onto his forehead. She flushed and scolded herself for even having such thoughts. She was a married woman. *Gosh, I almost said happily.*

On her way to the Jag, her mind wandered back to high school with the captain of the basketball team and the first love of her life. What had happened to cause their breakup? She couldn't remember.

Even though she'd seen Bob around town from time to time, they barely acknowledged each other. They would nod or wave. What was different about tonight?

Well, why worry about something that can lead nowhere? Might as well go home, since the ATM is now guarded by crime scene tape. Nuts, I can't go to breakfast tomorrow. During lunchtime, I have to go to the police station. That'll be a waste of time for sure.

Climbing into the Jag, she couldn't help wondering if Bob would be at the station tomorrow. She glanced at her watch. *Crap, Jim will be furious.*

Chapter Two

"I'm home." Trish shook out the umbrella at the front door and stuck it in its stand next to the roll-top desk in the sprawling foyer.

Jim Morgan peeked around the kitchen wall with a sour look on his face. "Where've you been?"

"Went to the ATM. Didn't you get my message? I needed some cash for tomorrow."

"Yeah, I got it. I'm hungry. What's for supper?"

"I really don't feel like fixing anything tonight. Could we just have a sandwich?"

Jim walked down the hall toward Trish, a grin spreading under his meticulously trimmed moustache. "Aw, Trish, I was counting on some fried chicken. That won't take too long, will it?"

Trish fought the anger welling up inside. "Jim, something happened at the ATM. I'm kinda shook up."

"What was that?" He leaned against the doorway, gnawing on a piece of provolone.

"I found an injured woman next to the bank. She'd been beaten and left for dead."

"Good Lord! I guess that's why you're so wet." Jim's expression didn't change. He ran a finger along her cheek and she shivered. "Well, it's all over now, sweetie. Let's have something to eat. Come on. It'll do you good to busy yourself in the kitchen." He took her arm and tried to lead her down the hall.

Maybe it was the trauma she'd been through or the weariness of being mindful of how Jim would react, but Trish surprised herself by snatching her arm away. Beads of water sprayed the hallway. "You aren't listening. I don't want to cook. I've had a traumatic experience. I'm cold and wet. I'm going up to shower and then go to bed."

Jim stood silently, his arm frozen in the position it had been in when she jerked away. His eyes narrowed and his smile disappeared. "I guess I can find something myself. But, dear, don't ever pull away from me like that again." Slowly his 6-foot-3 frame headed to the kitchen.

Trish breathed a sigh of relief and hung her sopping coat on the back of Jim's prized Louis the Fourteenth desk chair. *Screw the chair*. Her heart fluttered and she knew her blood pressure was elevated from the events of the evening and then the confrontation. Her breath caught in her chest when she spotted some dark brown splotches on her fuchsia leather coat.

Oh, I hope that woman's okay.
****

The hot shower refreshed her. She quickly toweled off and put on the flannel nightgown Jim hated. She sat down at her makeup table to dry her hair and started when Jim appeared in the mirror, then touched her shoulder. "Feel better now?"

"Much, thank you. I'm sorry I was so short earlier, but I was really shaken by what happened. I have to go to the police station tomorrow and give a statement."

"You must have been upset because you forgot and put your jacket on the Louis Fourteenth. I found it in time to keep it from causing damage." His hand rested on her shoulder and he squeezed hard causing her to move her head toward the pain. "We must be more careful."

Trish gasped. "I'm sorry. I wasn't thinking." Finally, he eased the pressure. She reached up and massaged her neck.

Jim's fingers slowly traced circles on her neck and met her hand. She fought the urge to pull away. "I forgive you. Let me get a shower and I'll give you a foot rub. That always relaxes you."

And always leads to something else. No thanks. Not tonight.

"I'm fine. I just want to go to bed and forget about this whole thing."

"Oh, all right. Have it your way." His voice carried that tone again. Anger lurking beneath the surface. But he left, and she crawled into bed, thankful for the soft down comforter that settled around her tense body.

I never wanted that damn chair anyway.

Later, she felt the bed move as Jim tugged the covers over himself. He moved closer to her and touched her arm. "You awake?"

She held her breath and did not move, tightening her eyes with every muscle available. Her heart thundered and she thought Jim must be able to hear it.

"Good night, dear."

Soon Jim's familiar snoring filled the room and she relaxed. She tried to regulate her breathing and prayed sleep would come. The bloody scene around the bank haunted her. Sometime in the wee hours of the morning, she finally slept.

****

After Jim left for work, Trish ate a leisurely breakfast. She hated she hadn't been able to draw money from the bank last night and had to miss breakfast with the girls. She really needed to talk to someone about last night. But admitting she had little or no money embarrassed her. She'd borrowed from them too much already. No use asking Jim. The checkbook never left his sight; he didn't like what she spent as it was. He insisted on receiving her paycheck every two weeks. At first, she accepted his claim it was only to keep things together. But it soon proved to be another form of control.

Trish tidied up the kitchen and in her haste, dropped a glass. It shattered on the ceramic floor. *Shit! Why does this always happen when I'm in a hurry?* She carefully gathered up the broken pieces. Then she stomped upstairs to finish getting dressed for work. Nothing in the closet seemed appropriate. Finally, she threw on a wool sweater and skirt. *What the hell is appropriate for the police?* She had to make several trips upstairs for things she forgot. She seemed to be wandering around in someone else's body.

Grabbing her purse from the dresser, she opened it to make sure her cell phone was charged. Her hand stilled. *What's this? I don't remember putting a DVD in my purse.* Trish plucked the disk from her purse.

Oh, my God. It's got blood on it. Where... The woman... She must have stuck it in my purse. But why? Not wanting to get anything on her clothes, she carried the disk down to the kitchen and dropped it into a plastic baggie, then put it back into her purse. *Probably got my fingerprints all over it now. Crap, look at the time. Sloan will have my hide.*

Chapter Three

As usual, Trish had to race to get to work on time since it had taken so long to leave the house. All the secretaries and assistants swarmed around her as she entered the law offices.

"There she is. Trish, Trish? We heard about what happened last night. It's all over the radio." Heather Samuels' usually smiling face wrinkled with concern. "You've got to tell us what went on, girl."

The women pressed in closer, nodding in eager agreement.

"Not a lot, really. I went to the ATM and heard a noise. It was a woman who had been injured. I called nine one one and that was that. Back off a little. I'm beginning to get claustrophobia here."

Heather's eyes opened so wide Trish thought her extra-long false eyelashes might stick to her eyebrows. "They just announced on the radio—the woman died last night. So you witnessed a murder."

"Oh, God, no. How awful. I'm so sorry for her." Tears welled in Trish's eyes.

Charity Taylor-Edwards smoothed her shoulder-length blonde locks. "Did you see who whacked her? Were you scared?"

Trish gave her a look of disdain. "No, I didn't see who whacked her. And I didn't witness a murder, I only found the victim." Trish moved toward her desk and the crowd followed.

Robert Sloan, junior partner and office manager, approached in his usual lethargic gait and windmilled his arms at the group. "Let's get back to work, everyone. We all have lots to do. Are you okay to work, Trish?" Sloan herded Heather away.

Heather, as she often did, puffed out her cheeks and waddled back to her desk. Sloan had not yet caught her mocking him. Behind his back she referred to him as "Moby" or the "Great White Whale." In a semblance of fairness, Mr. Sloan's chauvinism often failed to remain below the surface.

"I'm fine, Mr. Sloan. I have to be at the police station at noon for a statement. I don't think it should take too long."

"Take what time you need." Sloan crossed his arms, which because of his girth ended up being crossed wrists. "I would like to get that deposition on the Crane case finished today, though. It's due tomorrow, early."

"I'll stay late if I need to, sir."

"I knew I could count on you, Trish. I'm glad you had limited involvement in that business. Please try to keep the firm's name away from the press if you can. See you later."

The phone rang and Trish waved at Sloan as he walked away.

"Sloan, Walters, Walters, and Spitzer. This is Trish Morgan. How may I help you?"

Heather giggled. "You can fill me in on the details now that Moby is gone."

Trish looked around. Everyone but Heather busily conducted SWW&S's affairs. *I feel like a secret agent contacted by one of my spies.* "Heather, I've got a lot of work to do. I told you all about it just a minute ago."

"I know you. There's something you're holding back. You know I'm psychic. Spill it."

"If you're so psychic, why don't you tell me what it is?"

"Come on. I'll keep bugging you till you tell me."

"We'll talk at break time, if I can get this deposition done. Hang up and let me get at it."

"Meet me at ten-fifteen in the supply closet. You tell Heather all about it. No holding back."

"Goodbye, Heather." Trish replaced the receiver and leaned back in her chair. The disk in her purse had been bugging her. *Since that poor woman died, I'm the only one who knows about it. At least, I hope I'm the only one.* The hair on the nape of her neck rose. Suppose she wasn't the only one. That woman's death was not because of a robbery. The police had said she still wore her jewelry and her money was still in her purse. And Bob had found her ATM card. Apparently, someone went to extreme lengths to get it last night. Otherwise, why had they beaten that woman?

I'm just scaring myself with ridiculous notions. I'll give it to the police and be done with it.

Trish dove into her work. Thankfully, the first part of the morning flew by. She completed at least three-fourths of the deposition for Sloan, as well as handling a few other *emergencies*, as the lawyers called them. Thank goodness, she wouldn't have to stay late. Jim always got upset when she had to work past five. He'd call five or six times to make sure she was okay.

She walked to the supply closet at 10:15 looking over her shoulder for…she didn't know what or who.

Heather pulled her inside, closed the door, and flipped on the light. "This morning dragged on so slow, I couldn't stand it. I've been itching to get in here and talk. Okay, tell me. What are you holding back?" Heather's brown eyes bored into Trish's.

Trish feared everything in her mind would be revealed as clearly as if printed on a page. "I don't know how you do it, Heather. You really must be psychic. There is something else and it's worrying me a lot."

Heather practically jumped up and down. "I knew it. I knew it!"

Trish held up her hand. "Shhh. I don't want the whole town to know about this."

Heather stopped, closed her mouth, and gave a zip-it-up sign.

"When I got to the woman she was barely alive. There was so much blood." Trish couldn't stop the shiver that went through her. "Somehow she stuffed something into my purse when I wasn't looking. I found it this morning."

"Wow! What? Tell me what it was."

Trish stared at her and pursed her lips. Heather hunched her shoulders and gave one more zip-it-up signal. "It's a computer disk. No identifying label and it's a read only."

"What's on it?"

"I don't know and I won't know either. I'm giving it to the police."

"You aren't even going to take a little, tiny peek?" Heather looked incredulous and held her forefinger and thumb close together.

"No. I don't want to know what's on it. It may

16

have gotten a woman killed. I don't want that to happen to me. I'm going to get rid of it."

"Oh, come on now. It's important. It might be a national secret or something."

"Right." Trish snorted in derision. "Someone in Millvale has a top secret disk. Come on, Heather."

"Stranger things have happened. There's something else you need to think about. Whoever did this, if they're looking for the disk, might think you have it and you've seen what's on it."

It hit Trish between the eyes. Of course. It was in her possession. Who wouldn't want to look at what was on the disk? All morning Trish had thought long and hard about it herself. "Oh, God. You're right. Why didn't I think of that?"

"Hey, you've been stressed to the breaking point, seeing a murder and all. Anyone would be discombobulated. Even me. Now here's what we're going to do."

"Wait a minute. What's this 'we' business? I told you I'm getting rid of the disk."

Heather held out her hand. "Let me see it."

"No. I'm not letting it out of my sight. Not for a second. Besides, it's evidence. I feel like I should guard it or something."

"From me? Let me take a look at it and see what's there. Remember, I'm almost a PI."

"Yeah, from a correspondence school. And why you?" Trish couldn't hide the disdain in her voice.

"Come on, I have to see what's on it. Did you ever think I might be in danger from it, too?"

"You?"

"Who's your best friend? Just by knowing you, I

could be in trouble." Heather stood with her hands on her hips and determination written all over her face.

"I think you're stretching the connection a bit. When I give it to the police, your fingerprints would be on it."

"No, they wouldn't. You handle a DVD by the edge; they can't get a print that way. Part of my PI training, you know. Where's the disk?"

No use arguing with Heather. When she put her mind to something, nothing would stop her. *Besides I'm tired of dealing with the whole situation.* "Lower right hand drawer of my desk. It's in my purse in a freezer bag."

"You wait here. Give me a one-minute head start out of here. After I make a copy, I'll have it back in less than five minutes."

"I don't like this at all. Not one bit."

"Boy, I do. This is fun. My PI training's kicking in. Say, do you have a gun?"

"A gun?" Trish strangled a screech. "I most certainly do not. I'm as anti-gun as you can get."

"You may change your mind if this guy comes after you. You be careful. And go get a gun. Hey, I'll loan you one of mine."

"No. No guns."

"Let's see. You need one that's lightweight." Heather tapped Trish's shoulder. "My Glock twenty-two. It's a forty caliber. I'll get it on my lunch hour."

"I said no guns. Period!" Trish yelled.

"Okay, okay. Merely trying to help. It'll be around if you need it." Heather slipped out of the closet and surreptitiously looked around. She winked and pointed her forefinger with a thumb up at Trish in a mock shooting position.

One minute later, the door opened as Trish reached to grasp the knob. She practically jumped onto the third shelf of copy paper. Mr. Sloan walked in and nodded.

"Hope I didn't startle you. I thought I heard someone scream. Are you okay?"

"I'm fine. This whole thing last night has me on edge." She feigned looking at some boxes of toner as Mr. Sloan awkwardly reached around her, grabbed a bunch of sticky notepads, and left. She leaned on the shelving and tried to take a deep breath. *Oh, Lord, if only I could rewind my life back to a couple of days ago.*

Back at Trish's desk, Heather closed the desk drawer as she walked up.

"Needed some paper clips, Trish. Hope you don't mind." She said it a little too loudly from Trish's standpoint. She imagined everyone in the office would know something was up. She realized right then and there she wouldn't have the guts to be a PI. Heather flashed another thumbs up and sauntered off to her desk.

Trish sneaked a look in her purse at the disk encased in a plastic baggie.

I'll sure be glad to get rid of that stupid disk.

Chapter Four

Trish spent the rest of the morning finishing Sloan's deposition, then piddled at appearing busy. She couldn't help analyzing her situation. Should she call the police about the disk? Sure, Millvale's finest. Their idea of a tough night's work consisted of taking the mayor's son home after his latest fight. Bob seemed competent, but this was major.

She finally called and Mandy Pelikan, the receptionist, informed her no one was available and Bob wouldn't be back until noon. Okay, she'd meet him at noon and that would be that. The morning dragged on.

****

Trish had been glancing at the small digital clock on her desk off and on for the last twenty minutes. The green numerals had changed to 11:46. As she reached for her purse to head for the police station, her phone rang and she somehow kept from leaping on her desk.

"Spitzer, Walters, Walters, and Sloan. How may I help you?" Trish sat and again placed her purse on the desk.

"You can give me back my disk." The deep male voice seemed to crawl through her ear and into her brain.

"I beg your pardon?"

"You heard me, I want it back."

"Who is this?"

"Someone who doesn't want you to end up like Elizabeth."

Her heart thudded in her chest threatening to escape. "Listen, I don't know what you're talking about."

Anger filled his voice. "The disk."

"I don't have any disk."

"Don't be stupid. I know you have it and I want it."

"But I don't have it anymore. I gave it to the police." She couldn't think of anything else to say and hopefully this would get this maniac off her back.

"You idiot! You have to get it back."

Trish felt a drop of perspiration trickle down her back. "I can't do that. How am I going to steal the disk back from the police?"

"You're a smart girl. Just do it. You have twenty-four hours. Otherwise tomorrow, you're on a slab next to Elizabeth with a tag on your toe." The click on the phone seemed louder than usual. Trish sat there holding the phone and staring at the office water fountain. She dropped the receiver.

Heather walked up to her desk. "Trish, you look awfully pale. What's the matter?"

"Oh, nothing." Trish snagged a tissue from the box on her desk and dabbed her forehead.

"Okay, into the supply closet. Let's go." Heather pulled Trish out of her chair and pushed her all the way to the closet. Once inside she switched on the light and closed the door. "What happened?"

"I was getting ready to go to the police when my phone rang. This guy said I had to give him back the disk or he'd kill me." Trish felt the blood draining from her head. Her knees began to buckle. She leaned back against the door and shook her head.

Heather grabbed Trish's arms and gently shook her. "Steady, girl. Listen here. We've got to think this through. I'll bring you a gun at lunch."

"You will not. I'm not using a gun. End of that."

"I can teach you how to use it. Didn't take me long to learn at all."

"My uncle was killed by a careless friend handling a handgun. I swore I'd never pick one up and I won't change my mind now."

"Okay. Let me think." Heather leaned on the shelf filled with bottles of copy machine toner. "I got it. When I took the disk, I made a copy. I'll make another one and we can give it to this guy."

"When he gets it, he'll have no reason to keep me alive. In the movies they always end up dead. I don't think that's a good idea. Try to think of something feasible."

"All right. How about this? We agree to give this guy the disk. We arrange a meeting with him. When he gets there and you hand him the disk, I shoot him."

Her voice escalated. "You what!" This was unreal. *Were we really having a conversation about guns and secret disks and murder?*

"I, unlike you, have a gun. And I know how to use it. It's a beautiful three fifty-seven Magnum. It'll blast the guy to smithereens. Where I grew up, we took care of our own problems." Heather stood there with hands on hips and a matter-of-fact expression on her face. The statement had been uttered with no emotion or semblance of fear.

"This is not Chicago. This is Millvale for God's

sake. I don't want us to become the next Thelma and Louise. A meeting sounds like a bad idea. But how about if I tell him I'll leave it for him somewhere? Somewhere in a crowd of people."

"That's good. I think I saw that in a Dirty Harry movie once. Boy, this is fun, isn't it?"

"Heather, my idea of fun is a bowl of popcorn in front of a TV movie."

"Me too, with Brad Pitt draped all over me. Wooweee."

Trish looked at her watch. "Look, I've got to get to the police station. You need to get back to work, okay?"

"Oh, all right, Pilgrim." Heather left, attempting to mimic the walk of John Wayne, one of her favorite movie stars.

One minute she stood under the lone 60-watt bulb, which inadequately illuminated the small supply room, and the next she sat in her secretary's chair, staring at the fake fish in the aquarium on her computer screen. She couldn't believe she had been threatened. Trish Morgan, who never hurt a fly and avoided any possible confrontations, targeted by a murderer. What a nightmare!

How did my life become so screwed up? Suddenly, I'm in the middle of one of those cop shows on TV. Heather wants to outfit me for a S.W.A.T. team and have a showdown with a madman. I've got to get this disk to the police and be done with it.

As Trish readied herself to leave, Charity Taylor-Edwards hurried over to Trish's desk. Actually, more like sashayed. Charity, an ex-model, walked as though on a runway in New York. The guys loved it, but it drove Trish nuts. Charity placed both arms in Trish's in-box and leaned over. With her low-cut blouse, she displayed more cleavage than Trish cared to see.

"Trish? Is something wrong? You and Heather have been conspiring together all day. Does it have anything to do with last night?"

"We're planning something. It's no big deal."

Charity rose up to her full five-feet-seven inches and pulled her blonde hair behind her ear. "Sure, you are. I think it's got to do with your experience at the bank. Come on. You can tell me. I can keep a secret." In truth, Trish knew if the Chinese wanted to know something top secret, they should buy Charity a rum and Coke and get her talking about herself. Done deal.

"Just chatting, Charity. That's all."

Charity switched tactics. "Where were you at breakfast this morning? We had a great discussion about Luke. Isn't he a hunk? He's already asked me out."

"Good for you. I hope you two will be very happy. I missed breakfast because that darned ATM ate my card again. Listen I have to go to the police station and give them my statement. If I don't leave now, I'm going to be late." She gave Charity a forced smile. "They might send out a S.W.A.T. team to get me. Excuse me, will you? We'll talk later."

"Oh, sure. I'm on my way to the courthouse anyway. See ya." Charity twiddled her fingers at Trish and flounced away.

Trish sighed and stuffed some sensitive papers in her middle desk drawer, locked the desk, and picked up her purse. The police station was only two minutes away, so she probably wouldn't be late after all.

Heather waved a bright pink ink pen as she passed

her desk. "Give 'em hell, girl."

Trish looked back and snapped, "I'm only going to answer questions, not get booked. That PI course has you going nuts."

"Don't knock it. I might be able to save your life. I got an A in the course and they told me I'm a natural."

Trish stopped and turned around. "This is going to be the end of your stupid case, Heather. Drop it. I don't need anyone to save me."

"Uh huh, right. I'll be here when you need me."

Trish shook her head and scurried out the door.

Chapter Five

Trish closed the French doors of SWW&S and froze. *What am I doing? There's a madman on the loose and he has threatened me. What if he's waiting for me and I unconsciously walked outside alone?*

She looked up and down Main Street. Nothing seemed amiss, but how would she know? Traffic zipped past and only two people walked the sidewalks. She checked her purse to make sure her pepper spray was still accessible and decided to go those two blocks as fast as she could.

The Millvale Police Station occupied the corner of Main and Roosevelt. Beyond Main, the streets radiating from the center of town, east and west, were named for the presidents, and north to south were the states. Not an innovative bunch, the founding fathers, but it was hard to get lost in Millvale. And, of course, everybody knew everybody.

Trish turned up her coat collar and leaned into the early November wind, hurrying along North Main Street to finish her police interview. She smiled and nodded as she scurried past Mrs. Cooper, the nice lady from the bank, and then Mr. Parker from the Hair Raising Beauty Salon, who seemed more feminine than most of Trish's female friends.

Encountering no unfamiliar faces Trish finally arrived at the station steps. The old Carnegie building seemed even more imposing than normal as she sprinted up the stairs. The police had taken over ten years before when the city library moved into a brand new building with expanded parking on Washington Avenue.

Amanda Pelikan, wearing a parka over her Chicago Bulls sweatshirt, sat at the information desk, dabbing her perpetually red nose. She had an annoying habit of snorting instead of blowing.

Snort. "Hello Trish. How are you?" *Snort.*

"Fine, Mandy. I'm here to see Bob about last night."

"Oh, how about that?" *Snort.* "A murder here in Millvale. I may never use an ATM again." *Snort.* Amanda tossed the used tissue into her heaping wastebasket.

"I don't think we have a serial killer here, Mandy."

"So, you have your own investigation going, Trish?" Bob chimed in from behind, startling Trish.

"Well no, but I can't imagine anyone preying on the people of Millvale just out of the blue. Do you often sneak up behind innocent citizens?"

"Wasn't sneaking. I was here for our meeting. Come on back." Without waiting for her reply, he led the way through a clutter of desks and file cabinets toward his cubicle. "Careful. Watch your step. The city fathers use this area for storage so you have to negotiate the maze to get to our area."

Dresden-blue cubicles were a stark contrast to the bland gray color scheme and open architecture of the rest of the station décor. Though it seemed a crime to call it décor.

Bob motioned to a folding chair. "Have a seat,

Trish." He cleared an area of his desk by gathering a stack of papers and dropping them on the floor. "Want a cup of coffee grounds or a soda?"

She sat. "Sounds delicious, but no thanks. I want to get this over with."

Bob smiled and his dimples seemed to wink at her. "Our coffee's only good for staying awake on the night shift." She caught the scent of Old Spice.

Trish crossed her legs and nervously swung her right foot. "So what do you want to know about last night?" Perhaps diving into the interview would speed it up.

"Anything you can remember about arriving there. Did you see anyone around the ATM? Maybe a vehicle speeding away. Any detail that could help us nail this perp."

"I told you last night, I didn't see anyone or anything out of the ordinary." She sighed. "Like I said, I heard a moan and went to see if someone needed help. She did. But there was something else." Trish searched her purse and pulled out the plastic bag. "I think maybe she shoved this disk in my bag when I wasn't looking."

Bob stared at the disk as if it were a newly shrunken head. "Why didn't you tell me about it last night?"

"I knew nothing about it until this morning when I checked my purse. I tried calling but you were gone." Trish noticed she was sitting straighter in the chair and her voice had risen by an octave.

Bob held up his hand. "Take it easy, I wasn't accusing you of anything. Only curious. I'll get this to the lab. They'll give it to the state guys to analyze."

She leaned back in the chair and sighed. "Sorry.

I'm nervous. A man called me this morning wanting the disk back."

Bob leaned forward and raised his eyebrows. "He called you at work? What were his exact words?"

"I'm not sure I can repeat it verbatim. He said he knew I had the disk and wanted it back."

Bob placed the bag on his desk. "How'd he know where to get a hold of you?"

"You're the cop. You tell me."

Bob smiled. It softened his face and accentuated his dimples. "I had that coming, didn't I? One thing for sure, we need to get you some protection. I'm calling in the state police." He dialed and talked to the duty officer in Springfield. "They'll get back to me. In the meantime, did your caller say anything else?"

"He wants his disk back. I'm to steal it from you, since I told him I had already handed it over."

Bob rubbed his chin. "This may be the break we need."

"Can I ask a question?"

"Sure."

"Isn't there a video camera at the ATM?"

"We just finished looking at the tape."

"Were you able to identify the alleged assailant? I can't believe I'm saying something like that instead of typing it in a legal document."

"No, we couldn't. It was too dark, and with the light burned out, all we could make out was an arm and a hand grabbing the woman's arm and pulling her toward the alley. Trish, have you tried to look at what's on the disk?"

"Not at all. I put it in that baggie and then into my purse. The only time I touched it was when I wrapped it, so the disk wouldn't get damaged." *That's not really a lie. Just an omission about Heather copying it.*

"Good. You said last night you didn't know the victim. Now that you know her name is that still true?"

"What was her name again?"

"Elizabeth Thompson."

Trish shook her head. "Sorry, I don't recognize it. Who was she?"

"A new CPA in town, hired about two months ago by Elvis Tingle."

"Our meek little financial analyst? Do you think Elvis did it?"

"I don't think so. He lost big-time at a poker game last night, so he has an alibi."

"How do you know that?"

Bob sheepishly glanced at Trish. "I was there losing with him."

"Oh, great. Our police force involved in a gambling house."

"Nothing like that. A bunch of us play on Thursday nights. For fun. Nothing involving chunks of cash. Otherwise, I wouldn't be there. Can't lose more than twenty bucks a night. He also has another more prominent person who'll vouch for him being there. Our illustrious mayor. He was the big winner last night."

"Good Lord. The whole city staff is involved."

"It'll be front page news, I'm sure." He smiled. "On second thought, no, it won't, because the newspaper owner was there, too."

"A den of thieves. Well, what else do you need from me?" Not waiting for a reply, Trish stood up to go.

"Did Miss Thompson talk to you? Tell you anything?"

"No, she asked for help and then passed out."

Bob checked his notes. "That's all I need right now. I may follow up later if I have any other questions. If you think of something, give me a call."

"This guy on the phone wants me to steal the disk back from you. What should I do?"

"From what I hear the FBI will be taking over the investigation. Anyway, since they're now involved, you could tell your mystery caller the cops no longer have the disk. I guess now we wait till they let us know what we're supposed to do."

She started to leave.

"Oh, Trish?" She turned back. "It was nice talking to you again. It's been a long time. Would you like to have a cup of coffee sometime and talk?"

Trish's ears heated up. Whenever she was embarrassed, her ears let her, and everyone else, know. She always turned ten shades redder, maddeningly accentuating her freckles. "Do you think my husband would like that?"

Bob shrugged his shoulders. "I was just concerned this was causing you grief. Trying to offer some help. I apologize. I meant no harm."

Trish looked at his face and regretted her harshness. She could see hurt in his eyes. "Maybe I am a little out of sorts from this." She smiled. "No apology necessary. I'm sorry I snapped at you. That's not like me. We'll forget it happened." She waved goodbye.

Bob got up and grabbed his trooper cap. "Wait a minute. I'm walking you back to work. As a precaution."

"I'll be fine. No need." She wanted to accept but the offer of coffee made her a bit uncomfortable. However, remembering how rattled she was on her way to the station, she would feel better having an escort.

"I'm going and that's that. I told you I'd get you some protection. I don't like that phone call this morning. And I'm following you home tonight. It would be good for you to leave early. Vary your usual routine. Call and let me know when you're going home. I'll meet you in front of SWW&S. We'll come back to my office and I'll fill you in on what arrangements have been made."

"Suit yourself." Trish still felt flushed. Niggling in her mind was that her first inclination had been to say yes to his invitation to meet for coffee. They hurried through the station and Trish gave Mandy a pat on the shoulder on the way out. *Why do I suddenly feel like I'm in high school again?*

Trish practically ran back to SWW&S. Bob, taking long strides, seemed to be walking normally. He left after checking the lobby and told her a police car would be outside her home until they caught this guy. *Boy, that'll go over big with Jim.*

Trish thankfully noted Heather's empty desk when she returned. No more talk about this affair. It was over now. She wanted the workday to be over so she could go home to a nice quiet meal and a leisurely soak in a hot bath. Depending upon Jim's mood.

Heather suddenly appeared beside her, grabbing her arm. "We have to go. Come on." Once again, they disappeared into the supply closet.

Heather leaned against the door. "Well?"

"I finished my interview and gave Bob the disk.

It's over."

"No, it isn't. The killer still wants that disk."

"The police are going to get me some protection."

"Oh, that's going to work. Do the cops have any suspects?"

"No. Well, I don't know that they do. Bob wasn't really that free with any information."

"Do you think you can get that disk back?"

"No. Whatever you think of me, Heather, I'm not a thief. Especially stealing from the police. Are you nuts? Besides, didn't you hear me? The cops are handling this. Not us."

Heather leaned on the small shelf containing SWW&S ink pens. Each one to be accounted for and only given to paying customers. "Looks like the only choice you've got is to keep in sight of the police. I still think a gun would be a good idea."

She wasn't giving up. She was like a bulldog with a bone. *Just humor her.* "Okay, you carry one. Now, let's get back to work."

"On one condition. That I'm in on making this happen."

"You're in whether I want you in or not. Get going."

"You first. I don't want to be seen coming out of the closet with a woman." Heather giggled all the way back to her desk.

Chapter Six

Phinias Robert Sloan, junior partner, would be mortified if he had realized the entire staff at SWW&S knew his first name. His mother had wanted to honor her great grandfather by naming her son after him. But P. R. hated it—he even had all his certificates and diplomas redone to eliminate references to his first name. Office records of employment were also altered. But years ago, one of the associates had actually gone to the trouble of contacting the Montpelier, Vermont courthouse and had a copy of P. R. Sloan's birth certificate faxed to the office. Everyone in the office knew about it.

Trish felt uncomfortable approaching Mr. Sloan's office. He'd fondly say his door was always open, but in reality, it never was. One was expected to knock civilly and wait for his robust, "Enter!"

She rapped on the shiny mahogany door. It smelled of lemons.

"Enter!" Trish hesitated, then opened the door and peered in. The big man motioned irritably for her to come in all the way. Not usually a good sign. Sloan detested non-billable office interruptions. She crept in.

Mr. Sloan sat as ramrod straight in his burgundy leather chair as his 300-plus pounds would allow, and motioned for her to shut the door and sit down. Trish often wondered if the reason Sloan wanted to know who was at his door had to do with the comb over that refused to completely fill the bald patch on the top of his head. If someone came in unannounced and he had his head down that spot shone like a beacon.

"Trish, I'm very pleased with your work on the deposition and also the collecting of the brief in the Dellums' trial. Nice job. Now, was there something you wanted?"

"Yes, sir. The police asked that I return to the station as soon as possible. I wondered if I might leave early."

Sloan frowned. "More questions from them?"

"Something like that, yes."

"I hope you're not in any difficulty. Ha, ha." Obviously a forced laugh; his smile held no mirth.

She held her anger at his laughing off her trouble but still couldn't bring herself to reveal her true predicament. "Routine, is what they said. I have all my work caught up."

"No problem. You may leave at four forty-five."

Wow, a whole 15 minutes early. Gee, Phinias, I hope the firm can afford it. "Thanks, Mr. Sloan. I appreciate it. See you tomorrow."

"Good night, Trish."

You pompous twit. She glanced at her watch. *Still 30 minutes to kill before I can leave.*

Why had she used the word kill? She returned to her desk and sank into her chair. Trish sighed, picked up some papers at random, and studied them, not really focusing on the content. How could she concentrate on work when a killer was targeting her? *I'm surprised I'm not curled into a fetal position, lying on the floor sobbing my eyes out.* She absently selected the latest activity log from her inbox and checked to see what everyone in the office was doing.

Trish's work area, closest to the partner offices, denoted her position as assistant office manager. Ten years of service and an excellent work record had been rewarded with the top job in what everyone referred to as the "bullpen." Only partners had offices. At one time Trish had aspired to be a partner, but office politics and more than petty gender discrimination deflated that dream.

She'd finally finished her degree in September and was waiting to hear if she'd passed the bar exam. After that her choices looked rather slim, but she would accomplish her goal of becoming a lawyer. Something her late mom would have been proud of. Success had come easily to older sister Becky, a math whiz at 15, and now a project manager at NASA.

All associates were busily attacking the mountains of paperwork except Heather, who sat with compact in hand, looking back at Trish in the mirror. She pointed to the front door and turned her palm up. Trish shook her head and pointed to her watch, then held up four fingers twice and five fingers once, indicating when she could leave. Heather shrugged and resumed working.

At precisely 4:30, the murderer called back. Her stomach lurched at the sound of his voice.

"What's your cell phone number?" he snapped.

"Why do you want that?" The receiver shook as she tried to remain calm.

"I'm going to call you tomorrow to tell you what to do with the disk you're bringing me. Be at the Citizen's Office Building at ten sharp on the second floor beside the elevator. Alone and with the disk."

"I haven't got the disk." Trish gritted her teeth and her heart pounded. "I told you, it's at the police station."

"Then you'd better get to work to get it back. Now what's the number?"

"I'm not giving you my cell number."

"So you would rather meet face to face, up close and personal?"

Definitely something she didn't want to do. With a resolve to discontinue that phone contract as soon as possible, she gave him her number. Her phone went dead and she slowly hung up. Trish struggled not to cry. How could she rendezvous with a murderer? She could hand him the disk Heather copied and try to run away. *That's stupid. If he knows where I work, he probably knows where I live.* What brand of disk did she get that night? Sony. The copied disk was a Staples brand. He'd know the difference.

What am I going to do? What good is a hick town police department going to do me? Suddenly, Heather's idea of having a gun didn't seem so far-fetched.

Chapter Seven

At 4:40 Heather passed Trish's desk and laid a Sony DVD covertly on a stack of papers. The words 'extra copy' penned across a yellow sticky note attached to the disk told Trish all she needed to know. She looked up at Heather and mouthed, "thank you." Heather's only acknowledgement was a wave of a hand that held a clip full of bullets. Trish nearly passed out. She watched Heather stroll to her desk, sit down, and slip the ammo into her purse as calmly as if she had replaced a pack of her nasty cigarettes.

Taking a deep breath, Trish picked up the phone, called Bob, and told him she was on her way. He assured her he'd meet her in the lobby. She locked her desk at 4:44 and glanced at Sloan's office window. She could feel him watching and noting the fact she was leaving one minute early. Resisting the urge to daintily wave at the opaque glass, she turned and marched off to meet her escort.

True to his word, Bob was there, pacing in the foyer of the Cruickshank Business Complex, home to SWW&S, a small drug store, and the office of architect Nino Balamos.

He glanced up at her when the click of her high heels on the marble tiles caught his attention. He grinned sheepishly. "Been a slight change of plans."

"Change?"

Bob's gaze quickly shifted to where his shoe dug at two cracked floor tiles. "Uh, yeah, we need to go back to the station. The FBI is there ready to take over the investigation. I have no idea why."

Trish couldn't help but think Bob was reacting like a boy who'd been caught with his hand in the cookie jar. "You don't want them to?"

"I feel like Barney Fife, and they've taken my bullet away."

Trish smiled and touched his arm. "I appreciate your efforts, Bob, but I think we need as much help as we can get. At least, I feel that way. I'm not discounting your expertise, only thinking about the advantages of having more than one brain working on this problem."

"Well, if you put it that way, I'll accept it. Come on. Let's go see what they say."

Much to her surprise, Trish felt safer walking with Officer Bob Jenkins. He certainly presented an imposing figure in the tailored uniform. Still, she couldn't shake the sense of impending doom. Bob's eyes did a continual scan of the area around them for who knows what. When he pushed open the door, her heart seemed less likely to jump out of her throat inside the security of the police station. She scrutinized the street just traveled as if they had escaped the most dangerous swamp in the Everglades.

Bob's office was too small for the gathering they encountered, so they had moved to the office of Stan Landers, Chief of Police. Two men stood between Bob and the chief, one attired in a form-fitting, brown trooper uniform, the other wore a spotless, wrinkle-free dark suit. An official-looking badge hung from the jacket's breast pocket. The strangers exuded an air of authority in spite of the fact that at six feet, both still had to look up to Stan and Bob.

Chief Landers smiled and offered Trish a chair. "Good evening, Trish. Let me introduce everyone. That fellow there with the ugly flowered tie is Gordon Cheever, a lead investigator or something for the Chicago office of the FBI. To his right is Sam Shadonitz with the Illinois State Police." Each man nodded a greeting and pulled up a chair facing Trish.

Gordon Cheever smoothed his tie and leaned toward her. "Mrs. Morgan, we sympathize with your recent ordeal and appreciate your willingness to cooperate in the investigation. We'll try to make it as painless as possible. If you could, in your own words, take us through the events of last night."

Trish nervously clasped her hands and repeated her story for what seemed like the one hundredth time, answering each question succinctly.

"May I call home? My husband will be concerned."

Cheever sighed. "Someone give her a cell to use."

Bob handed her his phone.

Cheever held up his thumb and forefinger. "Make it a short one."

She had no problem keeping it short. Trish flipped the phone closed and returned it to Bob. She almost wished she hadn't called. Jim was disturbed and when she said she didn't know when she'd be home, he hung up. Later, Jim's interrogation would be much worse than the one she currently faced.

She returned to the question and answer session, actually relieved she would be away from home a while longer. The light from the video recorder blinded her as she spoke, reminding her of scenes of TV news conferences.

Cheever scratched his head through thick red hair and consulted his notes. "Stan said the killer has contacted you wanting the DVD returned."

"Yes, more than once." Bob and Stan shot concerned looks her way. "He called me before I left work. He wants me to steal the DVD back from Bob and then meet him to return it at ten a.m. tomorrow at the Citizens Building on the second floor. He has my cell phone number to contact me."

Sam Shadonitz interrupted. "How'd he get that?"

"I gave it to him. I had no choice but to cooperate." Shadonitz's eyebrows rose questioningly and she continued, "He knows where I work. I assume he knows where I live, too. I want this to be over. Then I can change my phone number and go back to being a nobody."

Cheever stood. "Mrs. Morgan, we need to huddle and talk this over. If you could wait a few more minutes?"

"I'll step outside."

Cheever gave a nod to Bob. "Officer Jenkins will go with you, just as a precaution." It was obvious; he was being dismissed from their planning session. They moved to the main squad room and sat down at one of the many empty desks.

Bob heaved a sigh. "Stan's not too happy with me lately."

"Why's that?" Trish was happy to be away from Cheever. And she was curious about Bob's statement.

"I've been offered a job with Homeland Security in Washington."

"That's wonderful, Bob. You should be very proud."

"It's a dream come true. I've always wanted to leave and do some real police work and now I'll be working with the best. Been trying for a couple of years."

"You must have some good credentials. They're careful who they hire."

"Spent ten years in the Air Force Air Police. I specialized in terrorist activities. Seems there's a greater need for that now."

"I'd think Stan would be happy for you."

"He'll have to work now." He raised his hand. "Don't get me wrong. He works, but I've been able to do the grunt stuff, freeing him for the administrative headaches. With me gone, he'll have to do it all and he's afraid they'll cut his budget, leaving no money for my replacement." He rubbed the end-of-the-day stubble on his chin. "I didn't tell him I was trying for the new job, thinking I probably wouldn't get it."

"I can see that might be a problem. When do you leave?"

"Not for a couple of months. They're allowing time to put things in order."

They talked for thirty minutes while the other cops conferred. Trish focused the conversation on the case, the weather, town politics, and SWW&S. Small talk about everything except their prior relationship. Finally, Stan called them back to his office.

Trish walked in thinking these four people held her suddenly fragile existence in their hands.

Chapter Eight

As Trish reentered the chief's office, Agent Cheever stood, while Trooper Shadonitz and Chief Landers half rose from their chairs.

"Mrs. Morgan, we've given this a lot of thought. I wanted to bring in an undercover woman from our office to substitute for you." Cheever placed his hands on the back of his chair and leaned over toward Trish. "We must assume the assailant knows what you look like. So you are our only hope of grabbing this guy. Please know we'll do everything in our power to protect you. However, you will be at risk. Do you understand?"

Trish's stomach rolled at the thought. She hesitated and then slowly nodded. "I'll do whatever you think best."

Cheever smiled. "Good. Good. We appreciate your willingness to help. Okay, here's the plan. A SWAT team dressed as civilians will be in place at the Citizen's Building tomorrow. You will have a copy of the original DVD and—"

Trish interrupted. "I have a copy already." She pulled a disk from her purse and handed it to Cheever. It still had Heather's sticky note attached.

"Excellent. Excellent. You've been thinking about this as well. I like that."

"I want this over with as quickly as possible. I had

43

planned to give the creep the copy and hand over the original to you."

Cheever raised his eyebrows. "That would be the prudent thing to do. Let us handle it."

The state policeman lifted his finger. "We've assigned a car to patrol your neighborhood twenty-four/seven."

Agent Cheever jumped in. "I think it is best if you come to work tomorrow as usual, then go to the Citizen's Building at ten sharp as he wants. Do you have any questions?"

"Yes, how about some protection for me when I go to meet him?"

Cheever was nodding. "Sorry, I forgot to include that. Plain-clothes officers will be stationed all along the way. Anything else?"

"Just one thing. How am I going to get any sleep tonight thinking about tomorrow?"

Cheever patted Trish on the shoulder. "I know it'll be tough. But after tomorrow, we'll have this guy, and you'll be free and clear. Think about that." He handed her the DVD, giving her an empathetic look. "I promise we'll give you every protection possible."

Trish placed the disk back in her purse and turned to go. Chief Landers opened his door and turned to Bob. "Jenkins will follow you home, Mrs. Morgan."

****

Seeing Bob's squad car following behind her made Trish uneasy. She'd never even had a traffic ticket and here a police car was trailing her home. She could see Bob, continually looking from side to side, watching for anything suspicious. *I hope I don't do anything stupid like run a red light with him behind me.*

44

Trish pulled the Jag into the driveway of her three-story Tudor home and turned off the ignition. She sat staring at the darkened house, her arms folded across the steering wheel. The only light came from Jim's office window. He was obviously so involved in his work he had forgotten to turn on the night-lights. With them on, the place was lit up like Christmas. With the lights, off the darkness was profound.

Jim's shadow moved in front of the window. *How had things gone so wrong for them? His protectiveness had been nice at first. Like he really cared. Heck, maybe he did. But now? His mental abuse and jealousy were becoming too much to handle. I have no idea how he'll react to this situation. With Bob bringing me home, that may set him off again.* Suddenly, a light came on and the shade drew back. She could see Jim's face. The unmistakable frown appeared and he dropped the curtain back against the window.

A finger tapping on her window caused her to jump. Bob stood outside in the rain probably wondering what she was doing. The rain battered the windshield, running in torrents down the glass surface. She waved at him and opened her door. As they ran to the front door, Trish fished in her purse for her key. No need. The door opened and Jim stared directly at Bob.

"I was wondering when you'd be home. How are you?"

"Fine, Mr. Morgan. Just a wee bit damp."

"Won't you come in?" Jim stepped back and held the door for them to enter. Both dripped water into spreading puddles. "To what do we owe the pleasure of your visit?"

"Doing my job. I was asked to escort Trish,

ah…Mrs. Morgan home."

"You were?" Jim looked at Trish.

She propped the umbrella against the wall and shimmied out of her coat. "I'll tell you about it when I get dry, Jim." She looked at the policeman. "Thanks for everything, Officer. I appreciate it very much."

Bob touched his trooper hat. "No problem. That's what I get paid for." He turned and jogged to his car as Jim slammed the front door.

"Explain, please." Both hands on hips accomplished the desired effect. She was frightened. Jim grasped the middle of her sweater and tightened the material until she could hardly breathe. "I told you to stay away from Jenkins, and here you are bringing him home with you."

She tried to push his hand away from her throat. "Please, I'm choking." The hand eased its hold a bit. At least she could take in air. "The police are keeping me under surveillance. There's a murderer loose, and he's after me."

He dropped his arm to his side. "Why didn't you tell me?"

Anger welled up in her and before she thought she blurted, "I tried yesterday, but you wouldn't listen."

Jim's eyes narrowed. "I'm sure I would have remembered about a murderer."

Trish put her palm on her chest and rubbed the place where Jim's fist had bored into her neck. "Please, let me get out of these clothes and I'll tell you all about it."

"All right. You go get dry and we'll have a talk." He turned and walked down the hall. "Yes, we have a few things to discuss."

Smudge

I can only guess what that'll be like. Thankful for the reprieve, she hurried upstairs to get cleaned up.

****

Jim sat at the dining room table Trish had inherited from her mother, the only thing she'd wanted from the estate. He was drinking a cup of coffee and smoking a cigarette. He knew she abhorred his smoking in the house and the possibility of putting any more burns on the tabletop. Trish took a chair opposite her husband.

He blew smoke her way; she clenched her teeth. "So, what's the story? I'm all ears." He leaned back in the chair and rested his elbow on the arm, holding the cigarette between his first two fingers. Ashes fluttered to the carpet.

"Why must you torment me like this?"

"Like what?" A smoke ring drifted to the ceiling.

Trying to keep her voice calm, she asked, "Is it something I've done?"

"We're not keeping score, but there is the matter of two nights without supper. This morning, I noticed a nasty scrape on the Jag's front tire. I specifically asked you not to fraternize with that cop and you defied me by bringing him here. To our house. You seem to be provoking me."

"Let's begin again. You asked about what is going on. Here's the whole story." Trish skipped no detail in recapping the murder investigation

Jim sat puffing away, stone-faced and silent until she finished.

"Quite a story. Did you know the woman? There was no mention of a name in the paper."

"No, she was some accountant with Elvis Tingle. Elizabeth something or other."

Jim sat upright. "Elizabeth Thompson?"

"Yes, I think that was the name. Do you know her?"

"I helped get her hired. I worked with her in Chicago for a while. Are the police investigating Elvis and his business?"

"I don't know. The FBI is involved and I haven't been privy to their plans. How well did you know her?"

"Just a co-worker. That's all." He got up, went into the living room, and pulled back the curtains. He looked outside and sighed. Then he returned and stood by Trish's chair. "Are the police out there for protection or surveillance?"

"They told me for protection. What's the matter?"

Jim waved his hand at her. "Nothing, nothing at all. Why don't you go up to bed? You must be exhausted. Get some sleep. I have some work to do, and then I'll come to bed. Good night." He left and she heard him take the steps up to his office two at a time.

What was that all about? He never even finished his tirade about no supper. That had never happened before. When he grabbed me, his eyes were filled with rage. Would he really hurt me?

Well, I'm not going to miss a chance to get a good night's sleep. At least I hope I can sleep. I'm not looking forward to tomorrow, that's for sure.

Chapter Nine

Trish opened the familiar door which had Spitzer, Walters, Walters, & Sloan Attorneys-at-law stenciled on the smoky glass window, feeling the same way she had her first day of work six years before. Only this time she really had her life on the line. She'd been thoroughly briefed, as Cheever had put it, on how to talk to the suspect. Though the term suspect seemed underkill to her. She shuddered. *Why use that word?*

She reached her desk, after acknowledging her co-workers with zombie-like greetings, and woodenly placed her purse in the bottom drawer as she had every day since day one. Dropping into her chair, Trish took a deep breath.

Can I actually deal with a murderer? What was I thinking? When they asked if I could do it, why had I said, "Oh sure?" Duh, I'm a civilian. Let the cops handle it. But no, my instinct to help kicked in. Stupid. Stupid. Stupid.

She sat back and surveyed her workplace. Four plush offices lined the wall behind Trish. The office of each higher-ranked partner was a bit more plush than the one before. The corner office belonged to the late Roland Spitzer. Ironically, the partnership still languished in court two years after his death. But the steady, lucrative work the firm received from its Chicago connections continued in spite of his death.

John Walters of Chicago, magna cum laude from Yale, and Travis Walters of Rolling Meadows, a Harvard grad and Rhodes Scholar were in a bitter fight to become the new head of the firm. Prospective clients assumed they were related. It was awkward when a client said they could see a resemblance. How they ever got together in the first place could serve as fodder for an Alfred Hitchcock movie.

The two surviving senior partners spent much of their time filing motions and counter motions vying for the top spot. The process continually delayed an ultimate settlement. Their business relationship had deteriorated into communication by memo using the office e-mail or messages via the staff. John Walters had latched onto Charity as his go-between. *Always did think he was the more lecherous of the two.* Travis Walters had selected Trish. And he had an annoying habit of snapping his fingers when he wanted her. *Someday I'm going to break one of those neatly manicured digits and slap him silly.*

She got up to get a cup of coffee at the employee lounge. *Huh. Some lounge.* A shelf at the back of the office containing a coffeemaker and cups. Underneath was a small cabinet to store lunches. No refrigerator.

Trish nearly fainted when Heather tapped her on the shoulder. "You okay, girl? You're mighty jumpy today."

"I'm fine. A little skittish is all."

"You better drag that entire pot along with you back to your desk. Uh, after you give me a cup, that is."

Both women ignored the hard and fast rule of no loitering in the lounge area. Heather took a big gulp from the cup Trish handed her. "Ow! Hot!" She waved her hand in front of her mouth. "So what's going on?"

"I'm not supposed to tell anyone."

"You've got to tell me. I'm part of the case."

"No, you're not. Doggone it this is not a case. I'm handing over the disk this morning and then I'm done with it."

"To the perp? The cops are lettin' you do it? Wow, that's cool. Need some company?"

Trish studied Heather's face. There was no sign of the question being one of the woman's put-ons. "No, you can't go with me. I shouldn't have said anything. You could get hurt."

"You can't? I could be your backup."

"Go sit down and get some work done. And I'm saying that in my official capacity as office supervisor."

"Okay, okay. Just tryin' to help." She pulled Trish's arm to get closer and whispered, "Did they give you a gun?"

"No." Trish blurted. "Get out of here." She gently pushed Heather toward her desk.

"I'm going. Stop shoving." She raised a finger that sported a silver nail emblazoned with the head of a leopard, as she walked away. "Remember, you can borrow mine any time."

Trish shook her head and turned to pick up her coffee. She was again shaken at the sight of Mr. Sloan beside her.

"I'm sorry, Trish. Did I startle you? I didn't mean to."

"No, no. I'm a bit out of sorts today."

"I like the way you handled Samuels." He picked up his coffee and started to leave.

Trish called after him. "Mr. Sloan, I need to take

some personal time this morning."

Sloan swirled back around. "Personal time? You know, we're awfully busy right now…"

Trish's eyes flashed. "Mr. Sloan, I've been here six years and have never missed a day, nor have I asked for personal time. This is not a request. This is notification."

Sloan stepped back. "Ah…well, okay. Yes, you're right. You go ahead and take some time. Yes, you do that. It's all right with me." He hurried off to his office.

Take that, you pompous twit. Trish retreated to her desk. *Did I just say that to my boss? I've never acted like that before. Must be from the stress. Although, it did feel pretty good.* She smiled. *I loved the look on his face and how he stuttered.*

The rest of the morning moved with agonizing slowness. She was torn between wanting it to go fast and cursing her involvement. She tried to get some work done, but it was useless. The rest of the office bustled with activity. *Come on clock, move.*

One-way glass windows, taking up half the wall, kept people from seeing into the offices, but allowed each partner a full view of office activity. All desks and tables faced away from the offices so the partners could instantly verify the work status of their employees, and no one fooled around. No one had fun at SWW&S.

Heather's desk sat two rows down from Trish. Charity occupied the desk in front of Trish, and her other breakfast buddy, Joan Landers, sat to Heather's left. The new "hunk," as Charity called him, sat in the desk closest to the front door. Luke Mattrick, a paralegal recently graduated from law school, answered phones, functioned as receptionist when a client arrived, and was the gofer for the remaining staff.

Trish wondered why she had stayed beyond the two years she had planned originally. Maybe it was time to think about moving on. If it meant Trish must leave Millvale, well, so be it. *And, perhaps an obsessive, domineering husband to boot.*

Chapter Ten

Trish glanced at the office clock for the umpteenth time. Thirteen after nine, two minutes slower than her watch. No doubt Mr. Sloan had set it that way on purpose.

"Good morning, Mrs. Morgan." Henry Davis, the local mailman, plopped the company mail on her desk pad.

"Hello, Henry. How you doing today?"

Henry scratched his head. "My psoriasis is acting up today, but I'm okay."

His red hair spilled out from under his mailman cap in all directions. Trish wondered if a good shampooing might be in order to alleviate the problem.

Henry had been delivering the mail since Trish had been with the company. He was an oddball, but always pleasant. Trish had long ago given up trying to carry on a normal conversation with him. It always turned to politics or religion—Henry was far right of the Grand Dragon of the Ku Klux Klan. And he was rabidly passionate about both subjects.

"Things going well with you, Mrs. M?"

"Just fine, thanks."

He shuffled his feet, clearly ready to discuss some left-wing perversion. "Did ya hear what the Dems are wanting now?"

"No, I haven't heard the news this morning, but I

really must get some work done. I have loads to do."

Henry leaned down, still scratching. "I'll tell ya tomorrow. It's going to bring the U. S. of A. to its knees. It is for sure. Every American needs to know…" He continued mumbling as he walked out the door and Trish heaved a sigh of relief. A sense of dread swept over her as she reminded herself not to be at her desk this time tomorrow. One thing was positive; Henry was always at the office at 9:20 a.m. every workday. At least it was 9:20 by her watch.

Poor Henry. Trish couldn't help feeling sorry for him in spite of his over-the-top views. He'd lost his wife and both children in an automobile accident three years before. His whole demeanor had changed from that of a happy-go-lucky pleasant guy to a deeply depressed, somewhat paranoid, man who believed the government was out to get him.

His slovenly dress and appearance were also a complete about-face. He had been, if not good looking, at least attractive. At six-foot-two with a good build and no sign of a paunch, he would have had no trouble dating some of Trish's single friends. More than one of them had remarked they enjoyed watching Henry walk away when he was wearing his mailman shorts during the hot summer months. But now Henry had withdrawn from the world. Trish had tried to hook him up with a couple of dates, but her matchmaking efforts fell on deaf ears. *So sad.*

The SWW&S clock on the wall ticked to 9:43. Trish put away the papers she had been staring at for the last ten minutes. She pushed back in her chair and sat for a minute trying to ratchet up the courage to confront a killer.

The butterfly dance in her stomach began again. She'd awakened off and on all night, dreading the confrontation today. *No use prolonging this anymore. Might as well dive in and get it over with.*

She grabbed her purse from the lower drawer of her desk and checked to see that the disk was still inside.

Heather tried and failed to look innocent as she ambled up beside Trish. She looked away and talked out of the side of her mouth. "I loaded my best gun with hollow points. I made them myself. In that brown purse on the corner of my desk. There's no safety. Just point and shoot."

"Oh, how thoughtful of you. I'll just go out and blow him away." Trish clenched her teeth. "No guns, thank you."

"Only trying to help." Heather shrugged her shoulders and walked off.

Trish rushed out of the office. At the elevator, she took a deep breath and counted to ten. Those butterflies were jumping at full speed now. Blood pounded in her ears as the elevator sank to ground level. She stepped into the lobby of her office building and looked around. There was a man squeegeeing the windows. Was he one of the S.W.A.T. men? He didn't make eye contact. He wasn't one of the regular cleaning people so she assumed he was a policeman. It was marginally reassuring to know someone was there to watch over her.

Outside, the pedestrians scurried in both directions. She pulled her collar up against the cold wind and wished she had remembered her gloves. Trish acknowledged those she knew with a wave or nod, forcing herself to smile. She knew it probably looked fake, but it was the least she could do.

She covered the two blocks to the Citizens' Building quickly. At the old-fashioned revolving doors, she stopped and filled her lungs with cold, bracing air, squared her shoulders, and resolutely walked inside. At the elevator, a woman in a business suit carrying a briefcase eased up beside her and a man with an identical case moved behind her. They entered; Trish pushed the button for the third floor. Her fellow passengers made no move to select a different floor. They all stared up at the lights flickering first on two, then three. A bell dinged. The doors opened.

Trish stepped into the corridor. The man and woman stopped outside the office of Tim Hastings, DDS and began chatting. A black man guided a push broom down the marble hallway. *Is he the one? Is he the killer?* Trish's knees went weak. She steadied herself by putting her hand on the wall next to the elevator. It was cold as was everything else in that hallway. Apparently, the heat was on only in the individual offices.

The black man made a couple of trips up and down the hall, never looked directly at her. Probably one of the FBI people. Nervously, she got the disk out of her purse and cupped it in her hand. If he was the one, she wanted him to see the DVD. She watched as he made one more round trip. Nothing. Must not be him.

Okay, so we wait. Trish checked her watch. 9:51. Still nine minutes to go. She tried to whistle but her lips were too dry. The taste of coffee lay stale on her tongue. At 9:53, she realized she was tapping her foot and stopped. Then, looking up and down the corridor, she saw the man and woman were still talking in low voices outside the dentist's office. The push-broom-man was again making his rounds. Two other men exchanged places between the Chamber of Commerce office and the office of Barney Patterson, accountant.

The elevator bell rang. Trish wiped a fine mist of sweat from her palms. Old Mrs. Speagle emerged and nodded to Trish. "Hello, Mrs. Morgan. I'm off to help Dr. Hastings put his daughter through college." She pointed to an enlarged jaw and trudged through the door between the conversationalists.

Trish sighed and again looked at her wristwatch. 9:58. She wished it were 10. No maybe she didn't.

The old, dark-mahogany wood covering the walls deadened what little light came from the tall narrow windows at each end of the hallway. Until now, Trish had enjoyed the 1930s architecture of the building. Today, it seemed creepy and intimidating.

The cell phone ringing in the depths of her purse brought a catch in her breath. The man and woman to her left quit talking, the push-broom-man changed his route to draw closer to her from the right.

Trish dropped her purse and hastily retrieved it, pulling out the phone. "Hello?"

"I see you're on time. Good. Keep following my directions to the letter and you'll get out of this alive."

Trish shivered. "What do you want me to do? Where are you?"

His voice rose. "Never mind where I am. Is anyone with you?"

"Um, not with me but a couple of people are in the hallway."

"That would be the police. Where are you in

relation to the elevator?" Ah, he couldn't see her from wherever he was.

"Just in front, about three steps."

"Okay, here's what to do. Turn your back to the elevator."

"Done."

"Now take about ten steps to your left."

She went the distance and stopped. "I'm here."

"You should be in front of or close to a mail chute."

Trish turned and spotted an old plaque over a slot with the word 'Mail' in raised letters. "Yes, I am."

"Drop the disk in the slot and wait for further instructions."

Trish felt her hand shaking. Consciously not looking at the man with the broom, Trish slid the disk in the slot and waited 'til it hit bottom a few seconds later.

Would this man be true to his word and leave her alone? *God I hope so*. She turned and lifted the phone to her ear once again. "Okay, I did that."

No answer. "Hello, are you there?"

The man and woman were on their way to Trish as she spoke. She closed the phone and watched as three more men left the adjoining offices. One of them was Cheever.

"What happened, Mrs. Morgan?"

"I, ah, did what he told me. I put the disk in the mail chute."

"Damn!" Cheever stomped his foot. "Everyone downstairs. Find out where that chute empties. Hurry! Take the stairs."

Trish exhaled and punched the elevator button.

That went well. I'm cold, my nose is running, and I'm twitching with deflated energy. Suddenly, we've lost our bargaining chip, the disk, and probably the killer, too. Peachy, just peachy.

Chapter Eleven

The elevator door opened. Trish sighed with relief when Bob Jenkins hurried out.

"Sorry, Trish. Are you okay?"

"Sure. Just a little shaken. The cavalry stampeded down the stairs a couple of minutes ago."

"I came to give some protection in case you needed it." He took her arm and escorted her into the elevator.

Trish pulled away. "I don't think I need protecting anymore. The disk is gone."

"I want to be sure you're safe."

Bob didn't try to touch her again and Trish was thankful. His touch was electric. She couldn't allow herself any such distractions. She'd already been thinking about Bob more than she should have.

They reached the lobby and saw no sign of any police presence. In fact, the first floor bank and offices were empty as far as she could tell. They walked back to her workplace in silence. Bob kept his head moving, scanning the street for any perceived threat. Trish felt a bit more relaxed. The drama was over; she could go back to living her life, such as it was.

"Thanks for all your help in this. I've felt safer with you around."

"Doing my job, that's all." Bob never looked at Trish during their return to SWW&S. At the building, he held the door for her, nodded as she went inside, and quickly left. She decided to take the stairs to her office instead of the elevator. The exertion felt good; she took the steps two at a time.

It didn't bother her when Mr. Sloan glanced at his watch as she dropped her purse in the bottom desk drawer. She immediately dug into the stack of papers that had grown higher on her desk while she was gone. Sloan made one of his grunts of displeasure but retreated to his office, saying nothing about the time she'd missed.

The phone rang and Trish jumped, feeling her temperature rise. *What now?*

"So what happened?"

Trish let a sigh of exasperation escape. "Oh, Heather, absolutely nothing exciting. The guy asked me over the phone to drop the disk in a mail chute, and the cops took off looking for him. Haven't seen them since and hope I never do again."

"That's it? Damn. I thought somebody might get shot or something."

"Nope. Look, Heather, I've got tons of work to do and not enough time to do it. Can we talk later?"

"Guess so. How about grabbing some dinner at Abe's tonight?"

"You know how Jim feels about that. I didn't cook last night and he was not happy."

"You've got to tell him to kiss off every once in a while. Show him where the skillet is and let him do something for once."

Trish smiled and took a deep breath. "Easier said than done, I'm afraid. I'll take a rain check. Okay?"

"Well, okay. Max wants to take me out tonight. I guess I'll let him. But Trish, take some time for yourself. You've been through a lot lately. Promise me?"

"You're a good friend, Heather. Yes, I promise." She put down the phone; Heather gave her a thumbs-up while still holding the phone to her ear. It was Heather's way of convincing Sloan, in case he was watching, they were not talking to each other.

Trish took a very brief lunch break and got back to work quickly. The paper pile shrank as Trish processed each one efficiently and rapidly.

Chapter Twelve

The afternoon dragged on. No way could she concentrate. She shuffled papers. The no-brainers were completed but she saved those requiring more thought for a better day. Trish replayed yesterday's mailbox incident and shuddered at the thought of the danger she'd faced. Laying her head on the desk, she tried to hide the tears beginning to run down her cheeks. *Could this finally be over?*

"Hey you, what's the matter?" Heather, perfectly plucked eyebrows bent in a frown, stood over her

"Just attempting to get back to feeling normal again. It isn't working."

Her friend crossed her arms, obviously considering what to say, then raised a finger. "Okay, here's an idea. You and I go to Abe's for dinner tonight. We gobble a great meal and split a bottle of cabernet. Dutch treat, of course." Heather winked.

Trish couldn't help smiling. "I'd love to, but I'd be terrible company. Besides, what would Jim say?"

Heather leaned down and took Trish's face in her hands. "Who cares what he thinks? This is for you. Just us girls. You deserve a night to yourself."

She's right. I do deserve one. Jim can get his own supper for once. She nodded. "Abe's it is. Right after work."

Trish watched Heather walk back to her desk,

whistling. When the phone rang a few minutes later, she picked it up still in a daze.

"Hi, honey. How are you doing?" Jim only called her honey when he wanted something.

"I'm okay, but really tired." Hopefully, he'd get the message.

"That's good. Listen, I'm bringing a client home tonight for dinner. Could you fix that special coq au vin you excel at? It'll just be us and him and his wife. About seven should be when we'll be home."

Trish gritted her teeth. "No, Jim. I will not. Didn't you hear me? I'm exhausted. I've had a rough week. I'm going to dinner with Heather."

"My week was no picnic, either. This is a very important client. Our future may become brighter if I can reel him in. This one time only, dear." He never called her dear unless he was making a demand.

"I won't spend this evening in the kitchen." Silence followed. She could hear him breathing on the other end of the phone. Several seconds passed.

"I don't think I heard you correctly."

"Yes, you did. Let me spell it out for you. N - O. You want coq au vin, you fix it yourself. I hope your client enjoys it." She slammed the phone down and then noticed the collection of startled looks directed toward her by the entire office staff. "Sorry. Just having a bad day."

Anger welled up in her and she found herself shaking. She attempted to finish her work but it was hopeless. Much like her situation in life.

Chapter Thirteen

Abe's Place catered to the casual diner as well as the more upscale Chicago crowd. Separated by two carved mahogany doors, one side of the restaurant featured white tablecloths, impeccably dressed waiters, and expensive steaks and seafood. The casual, more boisterous side served ribs and burgers and featured a flashy, neon-lit bar.

Heather steered Trish into the elegant side. She gave the maitre d' a big smile. "Two please. Smoking."

Trish jerked Heather's arm and signaled the man. "Non-smoking please."

Heather shrugged.

Trish constantly railed against Heather's seemingly unconquerable nicotine habit, and when she could, even hid the cancer weeds. Heather then threatened to shoot her if the lost articles didn't turn up in five minutes. Fortunately, this time the gun remained in Heather's purse, if she in fact had it with her at all.

A slender man with a pencil-thin moustache wearing a neatly fitted tuxedo escorted them to a private booth. He placed linen napkins on their laps. "Good evening, ladies. I am Max, your host for tonight. Might I suggest a glass of our wine of the day to start you off? It's an excellent white Zinfandel guaranteed to tickle the taste buds." Trish couldn't place the accent. Maybe French.

Heather gave Trish no chance to answer. "That sounds yummy. We'll have a glass."

"Excellent." Max turned and headed for the wine cellar.

"Heather, I'm on a strict budget here. You didn't even ask the price of the wine."

"Don't sweat it, my girl. Max and I are old friends." She winked at Trish.

"Oh, no. Is this the guy you've been talking about?"

"Yep. He's new in town. From Montreal. I grade him at just below Brad. Not too far either." She giggled and they watched Max return with a dark green bottle. He poured a touch in Heather's glass. She swirled it around and sniffed it, then took a sip. "Oh, that is good, Max." She held up her glass.

Max took the glass, his hands lingering on Heather's fingers. He filled both glasses. "What about an appetizer for the beautiful ladies?" Trish had to admit he was smooth, and the accent was delightful.

Again Trish had no chance to speak. "We'll have the crab cakes, and would you bring some of that excellent sauce?"

"But of course." He winked at Heather. "Coming right up."

Max left and Trish again tried to reason with Heather. "While I love crab cakes, I know what they cost. Don't order anything else for me, please."

"This meal is on me. I want you to relax. Throw caution to the wind. Get drunk if you want. You deserve it after all you've been through. Besides, I get Max's discount, and it's a hefty one. Sit back and enjoy."

Trish had two glasses of wine. The crab cakes were divine. But she had no appetite, and finally convinced Heather she couldn't eat anything other than a salad. Heather, on the other hand, ordered a huge meal. Max left to place the rest of their order.

"Now tell me what upset you this afternoon. Don't leave anything out."

Before she knew it, Trish had related Jim's phone call that afternoon.

"So," Heather said with satisfaction, "there's some backbone in that body after all. Good for you. If it had been me that dirt bag would've been out on his ear a couple of years ago. You want me to go home with you after we eat?"

"No. I can handle it. I think. His client will probably still be there; he won't make a scene."

The two talked for more than an hour while Heather devoured a twelve-ounce T-bone steak with all the trimmings. Trish relaxed from the wine and the unloading of her troubles. *What a blessing to have a friend like Heather.*

Max attended to their every need, making sure Heather felt his touch or caught his wink.

Trish pointed to the plate containing a bare bone on the other side of the table. "I was afraid you'd gnaw on that before you were through."

Heather laughed. "If we'd been on the other side of Abe's, I wouldn't have used a fork at all." She leaned closer to the table, keeping her voice low. "I think you need to get away from that madman you're living with. Come to my house for a while 'til you can find a place of your own. I have plenty of room."

Trish shook her head. "What would your boyfriend

think?"

"Max wouldn't care. He's really a great guy. I've got an extra room."

Trish's eyebrows rose. "So, you're living together."

Heather nodded sheepishly. "For about three weeks. We seemed to hit it off. Wait 'til you hear him play."

"Play?"

"Yeah, that's how we met. He's in a jazz combo and plays a mean sax."

"Many thanks for the offer of a room, but I'd never intrude. You're right about getting away, though. Jim's gotten much worse recently."

"You need a protection order against him. That is if the Keystone Cops and the local DA have such a thing."

"Wait a minute. Bob has been very helpful and it's not fair to characterize him that way. Our police department may be small, but they're efficient. Bob has been asked to join the Homeland Security."

"Bob? Are we getting friendly with *Bob*?" Heather emphasized the name, mocking Trish by raising her eyebrows.

"We're only acquaintances. I knew him in high school."

"Biblically knew him?"

"Okay, that's enough. We dated, and that's all. I've never been to bed with him. I'd never consider it."

"Never is a long time. With a creep like Jim, no one would blame you."

"I would. That's just not me. Enough said about that."

Heather put her hands up. "I surrender. Would you like me to go home with you?"

"No. I'll be fine."

"What about missing the meal with the clients? Won't he be furious?"

"Yes, but I'm never allowed to actually participate. Even when a couple is invited, I'm to just serve and be quiet. He'll rant and rave when it's over. He'd rant and rave about something else anyway."

"Doesn't sound like much of a marriage to me. Time to unhitch."

"I know. I feel like a failure."

"He's the failure. Takes two going full out to make a lasting relationship. Anyway, my offer stands, even if you need me in the middle of the night."

"Thanks, Heather. You don't know how much I appreciate that."

The meal had been delicious, and in spite of her anxiety about going home to face Jim, Trish was relaxed. She watched the interplay between Heather and Max and envied their relationship. Max was thoughtful and sensitive. Obviously, he adored her.

Trish thought back to her early married years. Jim had been like that in the beginning. Little love notes left on the fridge or on her pillow. Flowers often found in a vase on the table in the foyer to ask forgiveness for an argument. She couldn't remember the last time that had happened. Now, Jim's temper always seethed just under the surface.

Heather's right. It's time to leave.

If I leave how will I get by? What kind of job could I get? In a few weeks, I'll have my license. Then I can get a different job and get away from Jim for good. But

I can't leave yet. I just hope I survive with everything else that's hitting me.

A touch on her arm brought her back to the restaurant. "You okay, Trish? I lost you for a moment there."

Trish nodded and fought back some tears. She used her bright red napkin to disguise wiping her tears and laid it beside her plate. "Thanks for this great meal, Heather. I needed to get away for a while. But I'd better head on home. I'm already pushing the envelope."

"No problem. Can't complain about the company or the dreamy waiter. And I meant what I said. You need me, I'm there. By the way, did you notice Bob has been sitting two booths behind you?"

"You're kidding." Trish took out her compact and pointed the mirror over her shoulder. "Good God! That's him. He's spying on me."

"Uh, I think he's being protective. Isn't that sweet?" Her smile widened.

"I'm leaving. Thanks again. See you tomorrow." Trish practically leaped out of her chair and hurried past the startled Bob.

"Trish. Trish, wait." Bob was pulling out his wallet and waving for a waiter.

She stopped two steps beyond his booth. "What's the idea here, officer?" Diners stopped eating and focused on the two.

Bob spoke through clenched teeth. "Look, I'm trying to keep you safe and have dinner at the same time. Please sit down and let me finish my meal. I promise I won't bite. Well, except this fine steak."

Somewhat mollified, Trish hesitated. After all, there was the matter of a killer on the loose. She sat opposite him. "I'm sorry. I'm a little out of sorts lately."

"I won't be long, then I can escort you home. I promised Cheever I'd keep you safe. Please don't get me in trouble with the Feds. I really want that Homeland Security job."

"All right. I guess it was rather silly to start out on my own."

"Well, a homicide is not a usual occurrence in Millvale. Besides, I have some news."

Chapter Fourteen

Bob took an inordinate amount of time chewing his food. Trish was about to burst wanting to know his news.

"Okay, okay, swallow. What is it?"

Bob held up his hand and Trish sighed. "Minute," he managed to say. He put down his fork and took a drink. "Cheever says they have an ID on the guy in the video. It was Gino 'Fat Boy' Marciano. Haven't yet found the body. He is a notorious mob boss in Detroit who moved to Chicago in the late 90s to escape death threats. Seems he was carving out a big swatch of territory on the North side and someone decided to reduce the competition."

"So how does that help us?"

Bob reached for a folder beside him and pulled out a grainy photo. "This is the hit man. A copy is being distributed throughout the bureau to try to get an ID. Have you ever seen him before?"

Trish squinted at the picture. It was no use. She couldn't imagine anyone being able to identify the person from such a bad print. "Sorry, all I see is the form of a thin man with indistinguishable features. Looks like he has a moustache, but that's about it."

"The FBI is trying to get a computer enhancement to improve the quality. When they do, I'll let you see it."

J.D. Webb

"I hope they can do something with it." Trish pursed her lips and sat back in the chair.

"Give me a couple of minutes to finish my coffee and we'll go. Okay?"

She nodded and sat through ten minutes of uncomfortable silence. Bob struggled to be conversational, but neither spoke much. Trish must have shifted in her chair a half dozen times before he paid his check and they left.

Once outside, they were pelted with huge raindrops. Bob smiled at her. "Seems every time we meet lately, it's raining. Where's your car?"

She pointed to the right. "Down about four cars. It's the Jag. My car's not done yet."

Bob followed her hand. "I see it. Do you have an umbrella?"

"Sure, in the car. It's okay, I can run. I won't melt." She started trotting. Bob appeared beside her, running with no apparent effort. He held a notebook over her head as they ran.

He helped her into the car. "I'll follow. Don't leave until you see me behind you. That's an order, ma'am." He slammed the door shut before she could answer, and he was off.

The trip home was uneventful. She actually felt better having those headlights centered in her rearview mirror. She pulled into her driveway and parked next to a new Cadillac STS. *Must be the prospective client.*

Bob drove around the cul-de-sac and waved at her as he sped off.

Bob is so nice. Wonder what it would be like to go home with Bob? Come on, Trish, You're a married woman, for heaven's sake.

Trish hurried up the stairs and fumbled with her keychain, promptly dropping it in a puddle. *Crap. One more thing to add to today's list of crap.* Consciously slowing down, she finally inserted her key. *What the hell? I'm already drenched.* She kicked off her shoes and pushed the remnants of her last hair appointment out of her eyes. The hall closet was so full she didn't try to wedge in her coat. Besides it was wet, so she dropped it on the floor and trudged down the hall dripping splotches of water in a trail behind her.

Okay, let's get this over with. She felt like she was heading to the firing squad. Her pulse quickened as she tried not to think about how Jim might mete out punishment for her latest transgressions. Conversation came from the library so she peeked in.

"Ah, there she is. This is my sweetheart I was telling you about. Trish, meet Mr. Marciano. Sal, this is my wife."

Trish's breath caught in her chest *Oh my God! The name of the guy on the DVD.* She fought the urge to gasp out loud. *Is he related or is it some bizarre coincidence?*

A robust man of thirty-something struggled out of one of the leather easy chairs and reached for her hand. "So pleased to make your acquaintance, Mrs. M. Jim has done nothing but brag on you all night long." His thickly curled, black hair was plastered in place with an ample amount of gel, and he smelled of expensive cologne.

"I'm happy to meet you, Mr. Marciano." She quickly looked at Jim. "I'm sorry for my lateness, dear. I was held up. Well not literally, of course." She giggled nervously. *How stupid was that? I'm suddenly a ditz.* "Is there anything I can get for you gentlemen?" She had to get out of there.

Each shook his head.

"We're fine." Jim came over and took her arm. He squeezed hard. "You go up and change your clothes. You're soaking wet. We'll be a while. We have some business to attend to."

Trish smiled through gritted teeth and subtly twisted her arm away. It was all she could do not to wince. "Fine, I'll see you later then. So nice to meet you, Mr. Marciano. Excuse me." She made a hasty exit and rushed upstairs. *Could that man be connected to the mob guy? What's he doing with Jim?*

She took a quick shower and changed into her flannel pajamas. Plopping down on her side of the bed, she rubbed her arm and made a vow. *There's only so much I can take. I'm out of here tomorrow.* She opened her door and listened. The murmur of voices continued downstairs.

She went to her closet and pulled out her large and mid-sized suitcases. She quickly gathered essentials and then looked at the emergency stash under the mattress, where she'd been hoarding what little money she could. It totaled $212. Not much to begin a new life. Well, it would have to do. *Funny, I don't feel sad, more relieved.*

Her hands shook as she stuck the money in a side pocket of her smaller case and looked around her bedroom of six years. *Huh, what do I want to take to remind me of this life? Got to take my family Bible. Nothing here is really mine. Sis has all the family heirlooms.* She remembered Jim saying he wouldn't have her family's "junk" lying around *his* house.

Everything else in the room had been Jim's idea or done with his insistence. Gentle insistence at first, then without even consulting her. The décor was masculine. Nothing feminine. Ships were the theme in the paintings. A heavy four-poster bed with the firm mattress Jim preferred. Pictures on the dresser were of Jim's family, except for the one of her parents which she would grab in the morning. Should she call her father? No, he had not approved of her marriage. How right he was. *Why couldn't I see it? Blind love, I guess. How could I be so damn gullible?*

Her mother had looked so healthy in that photo. Only two short months later, cancer had claimed another victim. Tears rolled down Trish's cheeks. *My life is a mess. A failed marriage, having conversations with a murderer, unfulfilling job.*

Trish sighed and prepared for bed. But first she stashed the suitcases in the back of the closet where they normally sat empty.

Chapter Fifteen

Time for a fresh start. Tomorrow, I escape.
The night passed, with Trish finally falling asleep and never knowing when Jim came to bed. When she woke the next morning, his side of the bed had been slept in, but he was gone. She threw on a robe and went downstairs to make coffee. A light snow had fallen, leaving a white-covered lawn, but only dampening the pavement.

She looked around the cul-de-sac and spotted the police vehicle parked in front of the empty Jarvis house. A lone figure relaxed in the driver's seat drinking something out of a thermos. Something had knocked over the Jarvis's For Sale sign.

When the coffee was ready, Trish sat at the kitchen table. She placed both elbows on the clear glass top and rested the steaming cup in both hands, trying to warm them in the cool early morning.

So many things to think about. What would Jim do when he discovered she had moved out? Would he even care? *God, last week I don't think that question would have entered my mind. Well, honestly maybe it had entered but not been acted upon.*

Where will I go? I hate to impose on Heather, especially now that she and Max are roommates. My sister in Houston has enough problems with her three kids. Besides I don't think I could live in that frenetic household.

What do I do about my job? I can't afford to quit, but if I stay Jim will be able to find me. If I can hold out for a few weeks, I'll have my law license and I can look for another job. That is, if I passed the bar exam.

Trish went to the small desk that held Jim's precious computer. She fumbled around for a pad of paper and pencil. One of the things Jim was always saying about her was her bad habit of making lists. Lists of everything. Now she was glad she had kept that habit.

The clock on the wall showed it was approaching seven a.m. Better make arrangements to take a sick day. She called Heather at home.

"'Lo?"

"Sorry, Heather. I know I'm calling early."

"No problem. What's up?"

"I'm leaving him today. I wonder if you'd tell Sloan I'm sick."

"Good for you. Anything else I can do? My offer is still open."

"I don't think so. I have to sort all this out first and then figure out where I'm going. I appreciate the offer. I may take you up on it, but only as a last resort. I don't want to mess you up, too."

"You won't. Stop that, Max. I'm on the phone."

"Listen, I'll let you go and talk to you later."

"Be well, Trish. I'm on your side."

Trish hung up and returned to her list. *Okay what's next to do? I should get a bank account in my name. Oh no, the ATM ate my card again so I need to get that back and see how much is in there. Whatever it is, it's mine now.*

The phone rang and Trish almost had a heart stoppage. She felt frozen to the chair. The answering machine picked up.

Jim's voice monotoned. "Leave your message after the beep."

"Mrs. Morgan, it's Officer Jenkins. I know it's early, but if you're there, please answer."

Trish relaxed. She was afraid Jim had called to check on her. She picked up the receiver. "I'm here, Officer. What is it?"

"Wanted to let you know I'll be escorting you to work. What time do you leave?"

Uh oh. Didn't think about that. Crap. "Uh, I'm not going to work today. I called in sick."

"Sick? What's the problem?"

"Nothing serious. An upset stomach. I'll be fine."

"I'll have to let the Feds know. Don't go anywhere."

"Don't worry, I won't." Trish hung up. She hated lying to Bob but she had important things to do that were none of his business.

Trish finished packing her suitcases and set them beside the kitchen door. First, she had to take care of the ATM card. It was after eight, so she called the bank and was told the lost card could be picked up any time. They apologized for the inconvenience.

Downtown Millvale was a long walk from Trish's house, but she had no choice. She slipped on one of Jim's parkas and a stocking cap, hoping she looked like a man—or at least not like herself. Stuffing her purse inside the coat, she struggled with the heavy suitcases. Trish carefully eased out the side door onto the driveway, noting thankfully she left no footprints leading away from the house.

The suitcases needed to be stored somewhere since they would be a dead giveaway. Jim had ordered a cord of wood for the fireplace this winter. It was piled next to the garage, covered by a bright-blue tarpaulin. She stowed the bags under the tarp.

She moved to the front of the house and peeked around the corner. The figure in the police car was watching two neighbor boys in the yard across the street making snowballs. She took the opportunity and hurried to the sidewalk leading downtown. Trish pulled her purse from her coat and tried to walk as normally as she could, hoping the cops, if they noticed, would consider her merely another pedestrian.

The brisk walk in the cold air invigorated her. Taking some initiative and being in control felt good. *I'm going to make this work.*

Three blocks from the bank, a car honking behind her brought her crashing back to reality. "Trish, is that you?" The Millvale police cruiser inched alongside her.

"Yes, it's me."

"So, the stomach ache go away already?"

She shrugged. Turning to the car she breathed on her hands to get some warmth. Bob motioned for her to get in the car. Resigned to her fate, she obliged. "How did you recognize me?"

"Why, with expert police work." Bob smiled at her. "Your purse is very distinctive. I couldn't help notice the huge silver chain strap. Remember, I brought it back to you that night from the alley?"

"Damn. I guess I'm not cut out to be sneaky."

"What's going on? You know you're putting yourself in danger by being alone."

"Can we get a cup of coffee somewhere private? I'll tell you."

"Okay. How about my office? It's quiet; the chief is out of town today. Although it's the same coffee we always have. Amanda hates coffee, and when she makes it, she does so as a statement."

"Fine."

They rode in quiet to the station. Both nodded at Amanda as they entered. Bob led Trish into the small conference room and closed the door. She sagged into a chair and tossed her purse on the table.

"Want some? Coffee?"

"Sure, thanks."

While he was gone, Trish pondered this new crimp in her plans. She could see no way out unless she 'fessed up and told Bob everything. Maybe he could help.

When he returned, he looked at her sympathetically, and she found herself spilling it all. Afterward, she realized there was something cathartic about that. Just the fact someone else knew what she was going through.

When she finished Bob took off his trooper hat and rubbed his head. "Wow. You have a lot on that plate of yours, lady." He sat and studied Trish for a few seconds, then sighed. "I shouldn't do this, but I'm going to help you—on one condition."

"Yes?"

"That I transport you where you're going. I'll not intrude. Think of me as your chauffeur. I'm doing this against my better judgment and probably will be pissing off the Feds when they find out. But you're not safe by yourself with a murderer on the loose."

Chapter Sixteen

Signs all over the Citizen's National Bank of Millvale boasted a celebration of 100 years of excellence. Trish smiled at Mr. Caulkins, the president, as she marched through the freshly painted lobby. She had convinced Bob to stay outside. After all, it had to be safe inside the bank.

A plaque identified the teller as Jennifer Brookins. "Good morning, Trish. How are you today?"

"Fine, Jen. I need to retrieve my ATM card."

"Ate it again, huh?"

Trish nodded. Jennifer awkwardly dismounted her tall stool. Trish knew the bank insisted upon high counters to make it easier for customers to conduct their business. Short tellers like Jennifer had difficulty getting on and off the chairs. "Give me a minute to get it." She left the teller area and disappeared into an office in the back of the bank. She returned shortly and handed Trish the card.

"Thanks. Uh, I need to make a withdrawal. Can you tell me what the balance is?" Trish noticed she was nervously tapping her foot and willed it to stop.

The teller typed on the keyboard and read the screen back. "Looks like two thousand, one hundred, nine dollars and forty-five cents."

Ignoring the lump in her throat, Trish drew herself to full height. "I want twenty-one hundred." She had

J.D. Webb

intended to clean out the account but that would take Jim's signature. A much better statement could be made by leaving a small amount in the bank.

Jen smiled. "Do you want it in cash or check?"

"Cash, please." Her heart beat so loudly she wondered if Jennifer could hear it. This was more money than she had hoped. Stuffing a cash-filled envelope into her purse, she headed back outside. She noticed the music playing over the speaker system.

****

Bob started to get out of his cruiser when Trish approached, but she motioned for him to stay seated. Once inside the car, she relaxed. It felt good to have some funds to rely on. Things didn't look as bleak. Not that everything was hunky-dory. Only a tiny bit less stressful. She could imagine how Jim would react to her leaving. And even worse that she had only left $9.45 in their account. Well, too bad. He had made it impossible to stay.

"Where to?" Bob had both hands on the wheel and a quizzical look on his face.

"I don't know. I have to find a place to live. I want to go to the credit union and open an account. Oh, I know. Ted's Garage. I want to see if my car is fixed."

"Ted's it is, then. You know, even if your car is ready, I'm still following you."

"I know. But I won't be using our good taxpayer money to do my errands. Besides, what if you have an emergency to respond to?"

"Nothing happens in Millvale."

"Duh, like a murder and the FBI all over the place?"

Bob laughed. "Okay, you got me there."

Neither spoke during the trip to the garage. The smell of Old Spice wafted throughout the car. Funny, on Jim, it would have been undesirable but on Bob it smelled…well, comfortable. Very masculine. Bob stared straight ahead as he drove. She wondered what he was thinking. Before she could speculate, they pulled into the driveway of Ted's.

Ted Bandy wiped his hands on a grimy towel as he walked over to the police car. "Hey, Bob." He squinted against the sun and shaded his eyes in a mock salute under the brim of a John Deere cap. "Is that you, Trish? What are you bein' hauled in for?" His belly, not quite covered by a T-shirt of an indeterminate color, jiggled as he laughed.

"Taking advantage of a lift, Ted. Is my car ready yet?"

"Finished her up a couple of minutes ago. Had a clogged carburetor."

"Can you send me a bill? I'm a little rushed today." *Let Jim pay for the repairs. Might as well go for the jugular. It's time he did something for me.*

"You got it. I'll have it brought out to you." Ted ambled off, whistling.

Bob touched Trish's arm. "This is none of my business, Trish, but is there anything going on I should know about? Is Jim abusive?"

She looked into Bob's eyes. She saw concern and sincerity there. "There's a lot of tension and mental anguish, I guess. He doesn't beat me or anything like that. But I-I am afraid of him. That's one of the reasons I'm leaving."

"If there is anything I can do, you holler. I mean that as a friend, not just a cop."

85

"I know. Thanks." Trish got out of the car and then leaned in, holding onto the door. "I appreciate your help."

"I'll be in your rearview mirror. Where are you headed next?"

Good question. She hadn't given it any more thought since early this morning. "I guess to find a place to live for a while. I'll try Miss Beverly's B&B."

"Be careful." The cruiser rolled backward and then pulled onto Pierce Street.

A red Escort zigged through the parking lot and skidded to a stop beside her. Ted jumped out and held the door open. "Purrin' like a kitten, ain't it? I replaced the air filter as well as giving the carburetor a good reaming. Should be fine to go now."

Trish nodded as she wadded up a plastic seat cover and tossed it in the back. She slid into the driver's seat, hooked up the seat belt, and waved at Ted as she headed to the B&B. A block down the street, the police car pulled in and kept a steady three car lengths behind.

****

The Valley View Bed & Breakfast, a Victorian three-story complete with white picket fence and pink impatiens lining the sidewalk, stood atop the highest point in Millvale. The house looked and smelled as if it had been freshly painted. A sign directed visitors to the back parking area. Trish parked in one of the four lined spaces and got out.

Beverly Williams bounded down the stairs and grabbed both of Trish's hands in hers. She squinted in the sun and smiled. Freckles and splotches of flour dotted the woman's thin face.

"Trisha, what a pleasant surprise. I was finishing

up a peach pie when I saw your car come up. Must be a month since I've seen you. How have you been?"

"Okay. Working too hard and that's about it. How's Jane doing?"

"That's right, you haven't heard. I have a new grandbaby. Justin Bradley. He's the prettiest baby you ever saw." Bev's eyes sparkled with excitement.

"How wonderful. That's three now, isn't it?"

"Yep, two boys and one girl. And my two babies here." She pointed to a large cage hanging from a metal stand where two tiny multicolored birds whistled and flitted between three perches. "Tweedle Dee and Tweedle Dum are my company and help me keep my sanity."

"They're beautiful, Bev. And they sound wonderful."

"They're zebra finches. They make this place alive. Say, what brings you here?"

"I need a room, Bev."

"A room? For you?" She leaned back and gave a sideways look.

"Yes, me. Not long. Only a short while."

Trish could tell Bev wanted to ask questions but instead gave her a sympathetic look and nodded. "A room it is. You can have your choice. I have a two-room suite upstairs or a one bedroom on the first floor."

"Uh, how much?"

"For you the upstairs is sixty dollars a night or three-seventy a week and the downstairs is fifty a night or three hundred a week. That's breakfast included."

"Does the one downstairs have a separate entrance?"

"Sure does, and a nice veranda to sit on as well."

"I'll take it for a week. I need to find an apartment."

"Great, let's move you in. Your luggage in the trunk?" Bev started toward the back of the car.

"No. I have to go get it."

Bev stopped and turned around. "Okay, let me get the key." She frowned and cleared her throat. "Uh, Trish. Are you okay?"

"I'm fine. I need to get away by myself for a bit."

"Sure. It'll be great having someone to talk to. Business has been slow lately. You wait here."

When she returned, she motioned for Trish to follow. They moved along the sidewalk to a small porch full of potted plants. A slatted swing drifted in the breeze; a table and matching chair completed the cozy nook. Bev inserted the key and opened the door. In the corner stood a huge four-poster bed covered with an obviously hand-made quilt. The six throw pillows, all in shades of red, filled the room with color. An old desk and chair in the opposite corner and a matching dresser completed the furnishings.

"This is perfect, Bev. I want to pay right now. Is cash okay?"

"Honey, this is a business that loves cash. But you really don't have to pay 'til the end of the week."

"No, I like to get things finalized quickly." She counted out three one-hundred dollar bills and handed them to her new landlady.

"I'll get you a receipt and bring it down. When would you like to have breakfast?"

"I have to be at work by eight. Is seven too early?"

"No problem. I'm an old farm wife so I'm up at five every morning anyway." She nudged Trish with her elbow. "Shucks, with the ailments I have, sometimes it's three or four."

"It's a date, then."

Bev started to leave and turned. Her features softened. "Trish, your life is none of my business, but if you ever feel the need to talk, I'm here. I remember you growing up and playing with my Janie. We had some talks back then. I am still here for you. That's all I'll say. It's up to you."

Trish patted Bev on the arm. "I'm truly grateful for that, Bev. When I'm ready, I'll take you up on your offer. Thanks."

Bev left and Trish took a minute to freshen up. Then she drove to her home and pulled in the driveway. She saw the startled look on the surveillance man's face and watched as Bob pulled up behind the officer's car. He got out and they talked. There was a heated conversation but she couldn't tell what was being said. She decided not to worry about it.

Trish peered in the garage window and was pleased to see Jim's car was not there. She went to the tarp, tugged her suitcases out, and heaved them into the trunk of her car. She considered writing a note to Jim, but knew that would only make him more incensed. Nothing more could be said.

In yesterday's yelling, both had expressed their true feelings. She shivered as she remembered the hate in Jim's eyes when she told him she didn't love him anymore. She had trembled and was fearful he would do something drastic. He said he would never give her a divorce. She'd told him it didn't matter—she knew she could legally get one anyway. He had stomped into his study and slammed the door in a wall-shaking crash.

Trish got into her car and headed back to the bed and breakfast with two police cars following. She trudged around to her door, lugging the suitcases, and dropped them on the porch. As she inserted her key, Bob took off, leaving the FBI man parked in front. Trish made a mental note to alert Bev about her company tomorrow at breakfast. She sat on the edge of the bed, looking around her new home.

Well, the first step has been taken. Now I just have to get out of this alive.

Chapter Seventeen

Fifteen minutes before the alarm would have buzzed at 6:30 a.m., three cardinals fluttering and twittering around a bird feeder wakened Trish. She stretched and kicked off the covers, relishing the first restful sleep she'd had in…well, she couldn't remember how long. A wonderful aroma of fresh coffee, bacon, and something toasted made Trish's stomach rumble and she took less time than normal getting ready for work. She realized she had eaten very lightly since her dinner with Heather.

The dining room was awash with fresh-cut flowers; the table was set for two with old-fashioned place settings. Three covered dishes rested on trivets. A large pot of coffee sat on a stand, beckoning her to sit. Bev's finches whistled and warbled in their cage responding to her attention on the trips to and from the kitchen.

Bev returned with a plate of toast in one hand and a butter dish in the other. "Morning, Trish. Did you sleep well?"

"I don't think I've had a better night's sleep in years. Thank you."

Bev beamed. "Sit yourself down and dig in. If you don't mind, I'd like to join you. Haven't had anyone to talk to for some time."

"Please do." Trish sat and dished up a portion of a delicious-looking egg casserole. Bev sat and bowed her head. Trish stopped and embarrassedly bowed her head as well. Nothing was spoken out loud, but Trish said a silent prayer of thanks that she was beginning the next chapter in her life. Trish had always gone to church, but it seemed lately she didn't have time to pray. Pastor Gardiner would say that was a cop-out.

They talked about Millvale politics, Trish's job, and her plans to go into private practice. Bev talked about her family and brought Trish up-to-date on some of her former friends who had moved away.

"We've scampered all around what I really want to talk to you about. Are you okay?"

"Yeah, I'm okay. I realized I made a mistake and now I'm correcting it."

"Leaving Jim Morgan is a big step. He won't be happy. I know that much about him. Used to babysit him and his older brother years ago. There were two opposites if I ever saw 'em. When Tyler got killed, Jim seemed to lose interest in school, friends, and even family. He went around with deep depression in his eyes."

Trish shrugged. "I knew him from college. He seemed okay for the first years we were married. Then his dad died and he became a different person. One I don't know and don't particularly like."

Bev pushed a stray silver lock from in front of her bifocals. "Been there, done that. My first husband was a mean cuss, 'til I fixed him. I accidentally bumped him with my fifty-two Nash Ambassador, twice. And I threatened him with some nasty stuff when he went to sleep." She chuckled and her eyes twinkled. "Sure became a changed man then. You don't have a Nash, but the Jaguar would do nicely."

"No, nothing like that. I cleaned out our account and moved away."

"Oh, that's good. If there's anything I can do, you let me know." Bev patted Trish's hand and gathered the empty plates. "How about pork chops and homemade applesauce for supper tonight?"

"Sounds great, but I have no idea when I'll be here. I missed work yesterday. I'll have a huge pile to dig through when I get there."

Bev spoke over her shoulder as she headed for the kitchen. "I'll save some for when you get here. Won't be a problem to heat up."

"Thanks, Bev. I'll see you tonight." She wasn't sure Bev heard. Pans and dishes clanked together in the kitchen. She headed back to her room to grab her purse and arrive at SWW&S a bit early.

Chapter Eighteen

Normally, Trish would have enjoyed the deep blue sky and mild temperatures. Not today. Her life was in upheaval, and she had a mountain of work to catch up on. She grabbed the office doorknob and started to insert her key.

"Good morning, Trish."

She jumped at the sound of Mr. Sloan's voice and dropped the key. "Oh, you startled me." She bent for the key and promptly butted heads with Sloan, who had bent down to help her. "Sorry." She rubbed the sore spot.

Now beet red, Sloan waved a hand and opened the door. "No problem. You're early today. Are you feeling okay?"

"Fine. The twenty-four hour flu, I guess. I came in to catch up on what I missed doing yesterday."

A touch of a smile tugged at the corners of his mouth. "Admirable. Admirable. I'll let you get to it. Um, would you make some coffee?"

She gave him a sidelong look. "Yes." At least he had asked, and that was a plus after some of their heated discussions about her office duties.

After preparing extra strong coffee, she returned to her desk, which contained a huge pile of documents. She grimaced. Several folders had been tagged with red sticky notes, indicating urgency. Separating those into a neat stack, she began to tackle the most pressing. She barely acknowledged her office partners when they arrived. Inquiries about her illness were answered with short sentences.

When Henry Davis, the mailman, cleared his throat at her desk, Trish remembered her plan to be absent when he arrived. In all the hubbub, she'd forgotten. "Hello, Henry."

"Got a minute, Mrs. M.?"

"I'm afraid I haven't this morning, Henry. I'm swamped and the alligators are nipping at my..." She paused. "...heels."

Henry's freckles darkened as a loud grunt erupted from him. "Hey, that's a good 'n', Mrs. M. It's real important to hear what the Dems are going to do. It affects our very lives. They got this bill they're puttin' in the Congress that will take away our right to bear arms as is in the Second Amendment."

"Henry, I have no time to discuss this. Can we do it another time, please?"

Henry snatched up his mailbag and marched off, loudly proclaiming over his shoulder she had better pay more attention to what the government was doing to them. Because he for one, wasn't going to stand for it.

Trish sighed and returned to her work. Ten minutes later, the phone rang.

"You gave me the wrong DVD. I want mine."

Trish clapped her hand over her mouth. *It's him. Shit.* She forced herself to take a couple of deep breaths. "What do you mean? I put it in the mail slot like you told me."

"No. The cops must have switched it on you. You get that DVD or someone close to you is dead." He yelled into the phone. "Get it tomorrow. I'll call and tell you where to deliver it. I don't care that you have a cop watching you. I can take him out whenever I want. Oh yes, I know you're staying at Miss Beverly's house so don't think you're safe."

Trish shivered and squeezed the phone tighter. When she looked up Jim, stood in front of her desk. "We need to talk. Now." He planted his hands on his hips.

She covered the phone with one hand. "I can't talk right now, Jim."

"Put the phone down."

Before she knew it, she had pressed the hold button. *Oh great. I just put a murderer on hold. Jeez.* "Jim, leave or I'll have you thrown out." She punched the hold button and was greeted with a stream of profanity the likes of which she'd never heard before.

"I'm sorry. I pushed the hold button in error. It won't happen again."

He was screaming now. "You damn bet ya it won't or you're toast! When you get to your room tonight, check the closet. I left you a present. Then get that DVD or you'll resemble my gift." The phone clicked. She leaned back into her chair, exhaling heavily.

Trish's heart seemed to leap into her throat. *My God, he's been in my room. What kind of present did he leave? I'd better call Bev and warn her.*

Jim cleared his throat. "I'm waiting. Where can we talk? Or do you want to do it here in front of everyone?"

Trish stood up, gritted her teeth, and leaned across her desk. "I just got off the phone with a killer. He threatened me. Do you think you're going to scare me with anything you can say? Now get your butt out of here. We're through. I've left for good. I'll send for the rest of my belongings."

She'd never seen her husband so perplexed. He stuffed his hands in his pockets. Slowly—very slowly—he turned and walked away, staring at Trish's fellow workers, who were openly gawking.

As the door closed behind Jim, Heather rose from her desk and hurried over to Trish, clapping her hands. "I've been waiting for over a year for you to get some backbone. Way to go!"

Shaking, Trish fell into her chair. "I talked to the murderer again. He wants his disk back. I think I'm going to be sick."

"No, you're not. Wait a minute." Heather ran to her desk and pulled out a thermos bottle. She grabbed a handkerchief out of her purse and shook some water onto it. "Here, put this on your head. You'll be fine." Heather slapped the wet rag on Trish's forehead and held it in place.

"I put him on hold. How could I do that?"

"You put the killer on hold? Oh, that's precious. I love it."

Trish shivered. "It's not funny. He said I was as good as dead."

"Honey, you need to come and stay with me. I have an extra gun or two. We'll take this sucker out if he dares come around."

Trish shook her head, along with Heather's hand. "Heather, will you get serious? I need some constructive suggestions from a friend. Not an invitation to a shootout."

"Sorry. But I grew up in a nasty part of Chicago

with my grandparents. We had shootouts every weekend. If it wasn't the druggies, it was the gangs. I know how to handle myself."

"Just the same, I'm going to the police right now and let them handle it."

"Want me to go with you for protection?"

"They have a man outside. I'll be fine. Thanks."

"I just wish this was over." She removed the cloth from her head and handed it to her friend. "Thanks for the offer of a place to stay. And yes for the offer to blow this guy away but I don't want you to get hurt."

"Offer still stands. My brother and one of my cousins were killed in a drive-by right in front of me when I was eleven. I vowed never to be afraid again. And I won't be." Heather winked and returned to her desk.

Trish sat for a minute. She thought about the last call from the killer. Something about his voice. His words echoed in her brain as she tried to sort through snippets of the morning conversations. No way to identify what message her mind was sending. Anyway, there were more important things to do. Like going to the police. *Lord, please let this end soon.*

****

The Millvale Police Station bustled with activity. The FBI had taken over half of the main floor. Bob Jenkins had been relocated to a desk in the far corner. He sat hunched over a computer screen and failed to see Trish until she cleared her throat.

"Oh, hi, Trish. Ah, I mean, Mrs. Morgan." He looked around sheepishly.

"I have something to report, Bob."

"Looks like you'll have to spill it out here in the

open. Agent Cheever has confiscated my humble abode." He lifted his hand toward his cubicle.

"Sorry for that."

"They didn't like my helping you escape 'their surveillance,' as they put it. They banished me to this area. I call it my penalty box." He smiled.

"I had another call from the killer. He said he wants his DVD, not the one we gave him. He apparently knows the difference in the disks."

"Crap. Come on over here and let's tell Cheever." They squeezed between desks and around mounds of papers to the chief's office where he and Cheever were in a heated conversation.

"We haven't got any money for your meals, Cheever. We're over our yearly budget now. I can't authorize anything else." He looked at Bob and Trish and raised his eyebrows. "Something we can do for you two?"

Bob pushed in front of Trish. "We need to see you both, in there." He pointed into Landers' office. The chief shrugged and he and Cheever led the foursome inside. Cheever headed for the chief's chair until he caught a glimpse of the expression on Landers' face.

Bob closed the office door and stood in front of the desk. No one sat. "Trish just got a call from the killer. He knows we switched the DVDs. He wants his back."

Cheever exhaled, puffing out his cheeks. "We can't go through another fiasco like the first one. Especially with a civilian. God, why didn't I use my law degree?"

Landers gave him a sneer. "We'd all have been better off if you had. Bob, take Mrs. Morgan out and get a statement. We'll give you a call when we figure this out."

Bob slammed his hand on the desk. "No! We're not going anywhere. The four of us are going to discuss it. I'm tired of being excluded. I have some expertise in these matters. I insist on being involved from now on. The more heads on this the better. Trish needs to be here because…let's face it, she's the key to nabbing this guy. Now, let's sit down and talk."

Chapter Nineteen

Tension hung in the room. Cheever and Landers exchanged looks, each waiting for the other to respond. An uncomfortable silence surrounded the group until Trish spoke.

"I may be out of line here, but shouldn't we all work together to get out of this mess? We all seem to be control people, everyone trying to do our own thing and we're getting nowhere."

Chief Landers expelled a huge sigh and plopped into his chair. "You're right, Mrs. Morgan. You're right."

"Please, call me Trish."

Cheever pointed his finger at her. "I'll agree, but I remind you, I want you under surveillance at all times. No more sneaking around without protection. It's for your own good."

"I promise to be good."

An hour later, Trish was back in her room. Cheever had called her boss and told him she would not be at work the rest of the day and would be there only part of the day tomorrow. Trish wished she could have heard the other end of that conversation.

A knock at her door startled her.

"Who is it?"

"Bev. I noticed you were home and I wondered if you were okay."

Trish opened the door. Mrs. Williams stood there, wiping her hands on a dishtowel. A worried look was etched on her face.

"I'm all right. Thank you for your concern, Bev. I'm taking a break today."

"Look, it's none of my business…but I see you all stressed out, a strange car's sitting in the street, and these old busybody bones are telling me something's going on. I want you to know if there's anything I can help with, you just holler."

Trish smiled and patted Bev on the shoulder. "You are a dear. I am dealing with a…situation right now. I hope it will be cleared up soon. Don't you worry."

"All right, if you say so. Hey, it's eleven thirty, and I'm making lunch. You're welcome to join me. If you want to talk, I'd enjoy the company. Since Harold passed, I've had no one to chatter at."

"Oh, I don't want to put you to any trouble."

"Trouble? What's trouble about a chicken salad sandwich and some homemade raspberry tea? Come on." She grabbed Trish's arm and dragged her toward the kitchen. "You sit down and I'll fix you right up. How about the bread toasted? It's wheat bread from Donally's Bakery."

"Sounds divine. Thanks."

Bev efficiently prepared and served Trish one of the best lunches she'd had in a great while. Most of the time, she was forced to grab fast food, gobbling it down to meet the thirty-minute lunch limit imposed by SWW&S. This was five-star to her.

Trish leaned back in her chair and sighed. "That was absolutely delicious, Bev. Thank you."

The older woman looked down at Trish through

bifocals as she refilled Trish's glass. "I'm glad you liked it. I only ask one favor for payment."

"What's that?"

Bev set the tea container loudly onto the table and plopped into her chair. "Tell me what's going on. I'd like to help. And yes, it's none of my business. I promise I'll not gossip. 'Sides, I hate gossips. Got some in our church. I won't have anything to do with them."

The woman's face radiated excitement. Trish thought for a moment. *I'm actually putting this lovely woman in jeopardy. She at least ought to be aware of the circumstances.* Before Trish knew it the whole story had tumbled out. Surprisingly, she felt better. Having Bev know what she was going through seemed comforting. While Trish related the story, Bev hung on every word, offering no more than a nod or short grunt.

When Trish finished Bev was shaking her head. "My, oh my. You've gotten into one hell of a mess, as my old pappy used to say. The FBI working right here in Millvale? I bet the chief is bustin' his buttons."

"Well, I wouldn't go that far, but he's certainly yanking Bob around on a short chain."

"Seems to me you should be getting paid for putting your life on the line."

"All I want is for it to be over. One other important thing, Bev. The killer knows I'm staying here, so watch yourself."

"Shucks, I'm eighty-three years old and lived a good life. I'm happy to get some excitement going on rather than occupyin' a rocker and snappin' beans." Her eyes sparkled. She pounded the table. "Great guns, I've got to find the twenty-two Harold used for hunting. You know, I'm a good shot. He taught me everything he knew 'bout shooting. That SOB comes around here, he'll get himself ventilated."

"No. No guns. You might shoot the FBI agent. My friend Heather has a thing about guns as well. What is it with you two?"

"I learned early on, I need to take care of myself if there ain't no man around. That's what I intend to do."

"Well, do it while I'm not here, okay?"

Bev patted Trish's hand. "Don't you fret none. I'm not yet senile. I promise to ask questions first, before I blow anybody away." She smiled, looking nothing like a gun-toting grandmother.

"Please, let the police handle it."

"Long as they do it on someone else's property."

The doorbell rang. Bev jumped out of her chair. "Damn, that scared me." She put her hand over her mouth. "I'm sorry for the cursing, Trish. Wonder who it could be."

A man's silhouette was framed through the lacy white curtain that covered the front door. While Bev hurried to answer the ring, Trish got up and moved to the kitchen doorway.

Bev lifted the curtain and then opened the door. Henry Davis, his mail sack over his shoulder, stood holding a package in his hands. "Pardon, Mrs. Williams. I didn't want this package to get wet. They're predicting rain this afternoon." He peeked past Bev and held up his right hand, twiddling his fingers at Trish. "Hello, Mrs. Morgan. You visiting Mrs. Williams?"

She returned his wave. "Actually, Henry, I'm living here for a while. Would you be able to have my mail forwarded to this address?"

"Sure, no problemo. Be happy to. I'll bring a form

to fill out. You ladies take care. Some bad stuff happening in Millvale these days." He handed the package to Bev and hustled down the front porch steps, whistling.

Bev closed the door and read the label on the box. "Oh, good. It's my new wig."

"You wear a wig?"

"Course I do. My hair's so fine you can see my scalp. So I wear a wig." She winked at Trish. "Was goin' to get one with long auburn hair and shake up George Washburn, the druggist. He's been after me for at least three years since Harold passed. But then I figured he'd get a heart attack and I'd be liable to his kin for his death." She slapped her thigh. "Sure would have liked to do it, though."

Trish giggled. She really liked this woman.

The two retreated to the kitchen where Bev opened the box. She was examining the wig when her doorbell clanged again. Trish heard voices at the front door, and then Bev appeared, followed by the man who had been sitting in the parked FBI surveillance car. He towered over Bev looking uncomfortable standing next to the kitchen table.

"Sorry, Mrs. Morgan. Agent Cheever asked for you return to the station for a bit."

"Why?"

The big man shifted his weight and shrugged. "Don't know, Ma'am. Just told me to fetch you."

"Fetch? Like a dog? Is he a complete idiot?"

"Not my field of expertise, ma'am." Trish thought she saw a hint of a smile.

"Oh, stop calling me ma'am. Sounds like I'm an old schoolmarm or something. My name is Trish."

"Whatever you say, Trish. We need to go right now or I will hear about it."

"Let me get my purse and my keys. I'm going in my car." She grabbed her bag off the dresser in her room and rejoined the agent.

"I'll be back soon, Bev."

Bev nodded and went to wash the dishes piled in the sink.

At least, I hope I'm back soon.

Chapter Twenty

"How much do you know about your husband's business, Trish?"

Agent Cheever's question hung in the air and she grappled with her answer. "I really don't know much about it. He works in Chicago for a brokerage firm. Why do you ask?"

"Are you familiar with any of his clients or business associates?" Cheever's brow was furrowed as he paced beside Trish's chair in Chief Landers' office. Bob Jenkins and Chief Landers stood at the back of the room.

"He often invites clients or associates over for dinner to discuss business." Trish felt her neck getting hot.

"Are you included in his business discussions?"

"Of course not. They are privileged conversations."

"Do you know a man named Sal Marciano?"

"I don't know him but there was a Mr. Marciano at our house for dinner a few days ago. Heavy-set man with slicked-back hair, nicely dressed. Is that the one?"

"Yes, that's him."

"What's all this about? Why all the questions?"

Cheever turned to face her. "Mr. Marciano is a brother of the man who was murdered on the DVD you found."

Trish caught her breath. "You suspect my husband

had something to do with this mess?"

Cheever made no move and was silent.

"I don't believe Jim is the kind of person who goes around shooting people. I really must question your insinuation."

"Now, Mrs. Morgan. We're not accusing your husband of anything. We're trying to catch a murderer. We had information that Marciano, the victim's brother, was at your home and we wanted to verify it."

"Where did you get that information?"

"I'm not at liberty to say."

"Why all the questions about my husband's business?"

"I'm merely following leads."

Trish shot out of her chair and got right in Cheever's face. "I thought we had an agreement to work together on this. Here you grill me about Jim and ask questions leading me to believe you think he's involved in something. I want to know what brought this about. And don't tell me it's just the fact we had guests for dinner."

Cheever held up the palms of his hands and backed away. "Hold on. As I said, we're following leads. One thing we are interested in is finding out if there is a connection between your husband's firm and Marciano."

Bob Jenkins stepped forward and eased Trish into her chair. "Trish, calm down. This whole thing is exploding into a major crime ring investigation. Your husband's company has been under investigation for a while."

Cheever cleared his throat and shook his head at Bob.

Jenkins twirled around and pointed his finger at the FBI man. "Look, Agent Cheever, Trish is putting herself on the line here. She's willing to help and we should be giving her the benefit of the doubt."

Bob sat next to Trish. "There have been allegations that Mantra Securities, Jim's company, launders money for the mob. There is no evidence at all Jim is involved, other than he works there. As far as we know, he's only dealing with a client."

"Oh, my God." Trish knew her eyes were twice their normal size.

Bob continued, "Sal Marciano has taken over his brother's…shall we say, dealings."

Trish slumped in her chair. "He was in my house. He seemed nice enough and very polite, though."

Bob chuckled. "These guys usually don't advertise their bad side to the general public."

She gave a vague wave of her hand. "I know. But it seems so bizarre. Too many coincidences to cope with."

Cheever leaned on the chief's desk. "Well, as long as we're spilling the beans here, we have another problem we'd like your help with. Your law firm is under retainer to handle Mantra Securities legal activities." He picked up a paper from the desk. "A Mr. John Walters is their attorney of record."

"He's one of the partners."

"Do you have access to his files?" Cheever didn't even blink when he dropped this bomb.

Trish narrowed her eyes. "If you think I'm sneaking around and copying confidential files for you, you've got another think coming."

Cheever wasn't done yet. "It may be the only way to clear your husband."

"Let me tell you something. If my husband is guilty of something, he should go to jail. I'm not going to help put him there. I have enough to worry about with a failing marriage, keeping my job, and getting out from under the thumb of a killer."

"I can't make you do it, but you'd be doing a great service to—"

Trish held up her hands. "Don't say it. Don't say I'd be doing a great service to my country. I'm as patriotic as the next person, but I'm not further jeopardizing my future. I'm sorry, I don't feel I have an obligation to do any more."

Cheever walked away. "Okay. All I ask is that you think it over."

"You people are something. First you tell me you don't want a civilian involved and now you want me to be an undercover informant." She shook her head.

"You would have our complete protection. Our people would be around you at all times."

"Like the guy who didn't see me leave my house the other day? That sure relieves my concern."

Bob laughed. "She's got you there, Cheever."

Cheever looked as if he wanted to pull out his service weapon and blow Bob away.

Chief Landers sat behind his desk and crossed his arms across his chest. "Let's see where we go from here. This won't get resolved if we continue to argue."

There were murmurs of agreement.

"Okay, we expect our guy to contact Trish tomorrow and set up a meeting to get the DVD. Has that been covered?

"We have a GPS tracker on Trish's car and a tap on her cell phone. We have four chase cars, and people ready to go when the call comes in. Everything is set." Cheever still had a stern look directed at Bob.

"Anything else we need to do?"

Cheever shook his head. "Not for tomorrow." He turned to Trish. "I'd like to, one more time, impress upon you the value you could add to this investigation. We're close to taking down one of the biggest crime families in Chicago. You have access to files that could wrap up three years worth of work."

"I understand what you're saying, but I have to consider my own welfare. I need this job and the benefits. I'm separating from my husband and have no other choice but to protect my career."

"You're leaving Mr. Morgan?"

"Correction, have left. I moved out yesterday."

"Well, there goes my next possibility. We wanted to get a look at some of Mr. Morgan's files. I understand he has an office at home."

Trish clenched her fists. "Mr. Cheever, do you actually think I would spy on my husband? He may not be the perfect partner, but I would never breach a trust I pledged to him. What kind of person do you take me for?"

"We need additional information. I didn't believe you would agree, but I had to ask—to cover all bases. Now we'll have to get a warrant and probably mess up the house a little."

"Mess up the house?"

"Yes, our searches are quite thorough. We even dig up the yards if there is cause. We look inside cushions and we look for hidden safes or storage areas under the floors. Things like that."

Trish remembered how much fun it was to be given

free rein to decorate the living room. It was the only time in their entire marriage she was allowed complete control. That was when she was living what she thought was the perfect life. She had a quick image of Jim standing in the middle of his spotless office watching the Feds rip it apart. It would serve him right after what he had put her through. But the idea of someone trashing the rest of her home pained her. Even though Jim could be a complete ass, she wasn't convinced he was a criminal. Maybe she could help find some evidence to clear him.

Trish sighed and said, "What kind of papers are you looking for?"

Cheever smiled and began compiling a list of who and what would interest the FBI.

****

An hour later, Bob escorted Trish to her car. "I know how hard it is for you to give in to Cheever. I admire your loyalty."

She stopped at her red Escort and unlocked the door. She looked up at Bob. "I think it was finally a way to get him off my back. In the back of my mind I wondered, what if Jim is really innocent? I may be divorcing him, and frankly he's an ass, but I don't want to see him go to jail for something he didn't do."

"What are you going to do?"

"Right now, I'm going to Beverly's for dinner. I've worked up a huge appetite." She sat behind the wheel and aimed the key at the ignition.

Bob closed her door and leaned in the window. "See you there."

Trish was so startled she dropped the keyless entry remote on the floorboard. "What do you mean?"

"Bev invited me for dinner."

"She what?"

"Didn't you know? She's my aunt. See ya." He hurried to his squad car and pulled up behind Trish's car, waiting for her to leave.

Trish sat momentarily paralyzed by this news. The conversation with Bev last night had included a short inquiry about Bob and Trish's former relationship. Trish had made it clear that was long ago past and forgotten. At least she thought she'd made it clear. Now Bob was suddenly invited to dinner.

Might be time to have a little heart-to-heart talk with Bev.

Chapter Twenty-One

Trish pulled into her parking spot at the Valley View Bed & Breakfast and shut off the Escort's engine. She was looking forward to a short nap to try to relieve a nasty tension headache. She closed the car door with her shoulder and trudged toward her apartment entrance. *What a day.*

The tap on her shoulder sent electric shock waves throughout her body and her purse dropped to the ground.

"Hello, Mrs. Morgan." Henry Davis stood right behind her, with his finger still poised above her shoulder.

"Shit, Henry. You almost scared the...well, never mind. Don't ever do that again."

Henry's face abruptly changed to one approaching tears. "Gee, I didn't mean ta scare ya. I brought this form for you to fill out for the Post Office." He shoved a large yellow postcard at Trish. "It's the official U.S. Post Office Change of Address Form. It needs to be filled out so I can get your mail delivery changed."

Trish inhaled deeply and accepted the form. "That was very nice of you. I'm sorry I jumped at you. It took me by surprise that someone was here."

"That's okay. I'm very quiet. When you get the form filled out, just leave it with Bev's outgoing and I'll take care of it. Oh," he winked. "Don't need no stamp. Save ya forty-four cents."

"I will. Thanks again."

Henry sauntered down the driveway, whistling "America the Beautiful."

Trish shook her head and went inside. The old-fashioned cuckoo clock on the wall chirped twice as she dropped her purse on the dresser. Kicking off her shoes, Trish sat on the bed's down comforter and rubbed the back of her calves. *That settles it. I'm getting some flats to wear at work. I don't care what anyone says.*

She flopped down in the middle of the rose pattern on the comforter and stared at the ceiling. White fan blades moved in a slow rotation and she closed her eyes anticipating a short nap as Trish tried to rid herself of negative thoughts. She folded her arms across her stomach and closed her eyes. She imagined an ocean scene with waves lapping, sea gulls soaring, and a summer breeze gently ruffling palm fronds as she walked by. Then the damn phone rang.

She yanked it out of her purse and threw open the case.

"What is it?"

"Did you find my present?"

Trish bolted upright. It was him. That voice, causing her to shiver.

"What present? Look, I'm getting tired of your games. What do we do next?"

"Look in your closet. A green shoebox."

"Why?"

He yelled, "Do it!"

Trish slowly crawled off the bed and approached the closet, her breath coming in short spurts. A green box lay on the floor. Her hands shook as she reached for the lid. Inside, nestled in tissue paper, was one of Bev's beloved finches, its neck obviously broken.

The phone tumbled to the floor as Trish ran to the bathroom and flung open the toilet lid. She didn't remember how long she sat next to the bowl with a cold washrag pressed to her head. Finally able to keep the bile down, she retrieved her phone and put it to her ear. No sound. He'd hung up.

Someone banged on her outside door. "Mrs. Morgan? Are you all right? It's the FBI. Please let me in."

"I'm okay. Just a minute." Trish wiped her face on the washcloth and tossed it in the bathroom sink.

The tall man at the door waved his badge and looked past her into the room. "Agent Peterson, ma'am. You sure you're okay? We heard the conversation. What was the present?"

Trish wiggled her finger toward the closet. "Shoebox."

He went into the bathroom and brought out a towel. Then, kneeling down, he carefully wrapped the box containing the carcass. Holding the evidence in front of him, he stood and walked out the door. "We'll take care of this for you. Don't worry about it."

She closed the door after him and leaned back against the frame. When the phone rang again she gritted her teeth. *What does the dufus want now?*

She screamed into the phone. "What kind of a freak are you?"

"I see I got my point across. I mean business, Mrs. Morgan. I want you at the bus station in ten minutes. In front of locker number fifty-two. Bring the DVD. I'll call." The phone went dead.

Chapter Twenty-Two

The crash outside Trish's room accompanied an anguished cry. Trish rushed to the kitchen. Bev stood holding the sides of the birdcage. A bag of groceries lay on the floor, a pool of milk puddling around her feet. A very nervous bird flitted around inside the cage.

Bev looked over her shoulder. "Where is my Dee? She's gone. I know I left the cage door closed."

Trish hurried to Bev's side, ignoring the white liquid seeping into her sandals, and hugged her close. "Bev, I'm sorry. I found Dee in my closet. A madman has been here! He's given me a bizarre message...I'm afraid Dee became the victim."

Bev looked up at Trish, her eyes brimming with tears. "Someone killed her? Who would be so cruel?"

"Some crazed, inhuman madman. I'm so sorry I've brought this into your home. I'd better find someplace else to live."

Bev pushed out of Trish's arms and ran a hand over her cheeks. "Nonsense. You'll do nothing of the kind. I'd like to meet up with this pervert and yank a knot in his drawers. No need for you to leave. You say he was here in the house?" Bev punched herself in the forehead. "Oh, of course, if he did away with Dee he had to be in here. And what's this about some guy leaving you a message?"

Trish sat with Bev and related the whole story. Bev

listened with growing horror. She shook her head in disbelief as Trish finished.

"Who'd have thought in little Millvale someone so evil could be a neighbor? What happened to Dee?"

"The FBI man took her for evidence. They said they'd take good care of her."

"You must think I'm a nut case, feeling so, for a little bird."

Trish waved her hand. "Our pets are a vital part of our family. We grieve for them as we would anyone else. I know. It's frightening but I hope this will be resolved soon." Trish looked at her watch. "Nuts! I only have four minutes to get to the bus station. Bev, you've got to be careful. The FBI is here. If you need them, call."

"Huh. Where were they when my baby was being mutilated? You don't mind me. I'm getting Harold's gun and making sure it's in good working condition."

Trish shrugged and left. She stopped in her room to grab her purse, checked to make sure the DVD was still there, and hurried out to the sidewalk. The same FBI man stood talking on his cell phone. "Got it, sir. No problem." He acknowledged Trish and pointed to his car. "Get in. We need to get to the bus terminal."

Trish didn't argue. The plain gray sedan's tires screeched before she could get her seatbelt fastened.

The downtown bus station certainly was not her choice of places to visit. Vagrants, the homeless, and crack heads used the building as a gathering place and in some cases, a refuge. The FBI man stayed out in front of the building and dialed his cell phone as Trish entered the terminal. By her watch, she had less than a minute to find locker fifty-two.

Ignoring the vacant stares and pleas for money for a meal, she hurried to a bank of lockers, found the locker in question, and stood in front of it, trying to look natural. But her knees shook and her palms were sweating. *What am I doing here? Why can't I just turn around and run out of this place? Where are the feds?*

No one in the vicinity looked like a policeman. A bearded man, who continually sniffed like he had a cold, kept peeking at her. He was rail-thin and appeared sickly. A black man dressed in baggy jeans and smeared sweatshirt leaned on a post about twenty feet away. Three other people, seeming to pay her no attention, either sat or wandered in the main waiting area off to Trish's left.

An announcement of the arrival of the bus for Evansville droned over the intercom. Exactly ten minutes had passed since her phone call. Nothing happened. Two more minutes and her cell chirped.

"Hello?"

"Good, you're there. This'll all be over in a couple of minutes. I know the cops are with you. Don't try to deny it. Here's what I want you to do. Taped to the top of the locker is a key. Get it and open the locker."

Trish felt the top of the locker and found the key. The locker opened. "Okay, I did that."

"Do you see a laptop in there?"

"Yes."

"It should be open. Press the start key."

"Done."

"When it boots up, put in the DVD."

"Okay, it's ready."

"Push the F11 key. You should see a phone number. The area code will be in letters."

"I see it."

"Read it to me."

"FOW five five five, six one nine oh."

"Fine, now hit F12."

She did, and the screen melted away. A panel appeared that read, "File deleted."

"Okay, done. Hello? Hello?"

"Hey! What…" Trish staggered and was pushed to the side as the black man she'd seen earlier rushed to the computer and began typing furiously on the keyboard.

They were joined by the thin man and Cheever, who appeared from the coffee shop. Cheever tapped the black man on the shoulder. "Did you get it?"

The man turned and shrugged. "Nope. He had the function buttons programmed to destroy the data on the hard drive and on the DVD. Everything's gone."

"Crap!" Cheever punched numbers on his phone and yelled at it. "Did you get a trace on the cell phone? …What do you mean he had some weird routing thing set up? Never mind. Damn it. Is nothing going to go right on this case?"

Trish leaned against the side of the lockers and tried to follow what was happening. She was so very tired of the subterfuge and the emotional rollercoaster.

"Agent Cheever, are you through with me? I want to go home and try to forget this ever happened."

Cheever waved his hand. "Sure, go on. Nothing else to do here. Taylor, take her back home. Uh, thanks for your assistance. Oh, there is one more thing. Can you repeat the number he gave you?"

"I think it was FOW five five five six oh one nine. No, it was six one nine oh. Yes, six one nine oh, I'm sure of it."

****

The short trip back to her room was silent. Trish walked up to her porch and turned to see the government car slowly pulling away from the curb, probably returning to the bus station.

I don't blame him. I wouldn't want to go back and face Cheever either. God, please let this be finally over.

She trudged up the stairs and unlocked her door. *Might as well go see if I can help Bev clean up her kitchen.* She went into the hall and stopped dead when she came to the open doorway.

The floor was clean. In fact, the whole kitchen was spotless. Bev sat on a kitchen chair, calmly cleaning a rifle.

Chapter Twenty-Three

Trish stepped into the kitchen. "Oh, Bev. There's no need for guns now. It's all over." She patted the woman on the arm. "I'm really sorry to put you through this. I feel terrible about Tweedle Dee."

Bev waved an oily cloth at her. "Not necessary to apologize. Just wish that no-account had tried something when I was here. He'd be pullin' buckshot out of his rump for years."

"Well, I'll say one thing. I'd hate to try putting something over on you. I came down to help clean up the kitchen but I see you've taken care of it already."

Bev smiled grimly. "Kept thinking about spilled milk as I was toweling it up. Gave me a chuckle. Why don't you go get some rest? Take a nap and relax. You've been through a lot. I have some very nice salmon steaks I'm going to fix Cajun style for dinner tonight. Come down and help me get rid of them. Won't take no for an answer."

Trish held up her hand. "Oh, for goodness sake. I can't do that. You've done so much for me as it is."

"Nonsense. I'm enjoying having someone to talk to and I love to cook. Now don't spoil my fun."

Trish grinned. "If you put it that way, how can I refuse?"

"You can't. Now git. Be back here at 6 sharp."

Actually her mouth was watering just listening to

Bev talk about dinner. She'd missed lunch and was suddenly starving.

****

Trish tried to lie back and nap but she failed to shut her mind down. Her phone rang, barely audible inside her purse. She sat up. *What now?*

"Yes?"

"Mrs. Morgan, it's Gordon Cheever. Do you have a minute?"

Crap, doesn't he ever give up? "What do you want now, Cheever? I thought we were through."

"Uh, not quite. I was wondering if you've had a chance to look for those papers?"

"You've got to be kidding me! When would I have had a chance to do that—even if I had the inclination?"

"I'm sorry. I realize you've been under a strain, but we have only one hope to finish the case and that's to get inside and gather evidence. I thought I'd give you one more opportunity before we execute our search warrant. It's up to you."

Trish sighed. The only fun she'd had in the last three years was to redecorate the living room of their house. The thought of the Feds ruining her efforts was too much to bear. "All right. I'm not going to be able to take a nap anyway. I'll go now. I don't need any help. Jim will be at work, and there aren't that many places to hide anything. I'll call if, and I do mean if, I find anything."

"Thank you. I truly appreciate it. I'll wait for your call." He hung up.

Trish glanced at the cuckoo clock. 5:35. She gathered her purse and went to tell Bev she'd have to take a rain check on dinner.

Chapter Twenty-Four

It seemed like months since Trish had been home. *Home. How odd that sounds now.*

The Tudor's driveway curved around the house leading to the garage. Trish pulled in front of the open double door and turned off the engine. *That's funny, Jim's car is here. Well, we have to talk. Might as well get it over with. The search can wait for a while.*

She squared her shoulders and marched up to the rear entrance. On the tiny back porch, she clawed through her purse, looking for the house key. Then she noticed the broken corner windowpane in the door. *Uh oh. Looks like Jim's temper did a number on the door again. I hope he's calmed down by now.*

Trish pushed gently on the door and it opened. She tiptoed through glass shards and stepped across the threshold. "Jim? Jim, are you home?"

Quiet was the response. Trish moved through the kitchen into the hallway. She stopped at the second door. Jim's office. She knocked. Goosebumps raced up her arms as she pushed open the door.

The normally spotless room was trashed. Paper littered the floor. Leather chairs with gutted cushions bore no resemblance to those purchased during her redecoration. Books pulled from shelves lay in heaps beside the mahogany cabinets. Jim lay face down across his desk.

Oh, God no! Trish knew even without the dark brown stain near his head that Jim was dead. Suddenly, the bile no longer could be contained; she bent over and threw up. *No, this cannot be happening.* She swallowed hard to try to keep from vomiting again.

Be calm. Don't panic. Hah, too late for that! Christ, what if the killer is still here? Her brain yelled at her. *Get out!* She backed from the office and raced down the hall. She slammed the back door. *Where are my car keys? There, still hanging in the keyhole.* She grabbed them and sprinted to her car.

Her hand shook so badly she couldn't insert her key into the ignition. She pounded the steering wheel. *Come on!* Thank God, the car finally started; she stomped on the gas.

Dumping the contents of her purse on the passenger seat, Trish wrestled to control the swerving car and dig out her cell from the pile. "Nine one one?" *Of course, you idiot, that's what I dialed.* "My husband has been murdered. Please send help." *Lord, who would have thought I'd ever be saying that?*

"Please remain calm, Miss. Where are you?"

"I'm in my car. I ran out of the house and started driving."

"I mean, where did this take place?"

Trish gave the 911 operator her name and address, and told her what she'd seen. When Trish finished her report she was told to stay on the line. Holding the phone in front of her, Trish peered through the windshield in disbelief. A stop sign, bent at an awkward angle, rested on the hood of her car. The car sat on the boulevard of her neighbor Harlan Fitzgerald, fully a half block from her home. Mrs. Fitzgerald, hands on hips, stood on her front porch spewing words Trish wouldn't wish to repeat about some prize flowers being ruined. *Why does my head hurt?*

Approaching sirens drowned out Mrs. Fitzgerald. Trish slumped in the driver's seat, unwilling and unable to move. *This can't be real. It's some horrible nightmare.* Her hand pressed against the side of her head to help ease the pain.

A Millvale police car, lights flashing and siren screaming, slid to a halt inches from her bumper. Bob Jenkins jumped out. "Trish, are you okay? I heard the report. What happened?"

Trish opened the car door and swung her legs out. She wobbled and steadied herself by leaning on the fender. "Jim's dead. In his office. I found him and ran to get away in case the murderer was still there. I guess I had an accident while phoning nine one one."

"Sit here on the curb. You've got a nasty bump on the side of your head." Bob looked around. "Was someone chasing you?"

"No. I went home to…well…to talk. I found him sprawled across his desk. The place had been ransacked. I got the heck out of there as fast as I could."

An ambulance pulled up and the paramedics surrounded Trish. After a quick examination, they advised her to go to the hospital for tests. They concluded she might have a concussion.

She was moved to a gurney and loaded into the ambulance. The blaring siren did nothing to stop her pounding headache. Questions flooded her mind. *Who would want to kill Jim? What are they looking for? Was it the same thing Cheever wanted? And most important, was she still in danger?*

Chapter Twenty-Five

"So, when are you getting out of here?" Heather picked up the TV remote and changed the channel.

"They say I can leave tomorrow. I'm only under observation." Trish grabbed the control and switched channels again.

"Heck, I'd like to be under observation by that cute doctor who was in here a few minutes ago. He sure gave you the once over."

"I'm not looking for a date. I've got other things to take care of."

"Oh, yeah. Trish, I'm real sorry about Jim. Even though he was a jerk, you never want anyone to be killed. Have they got any idea who did it yet?"

Trish sighed. "No. There were no fingerprints, no shell casings, and no evidence at all. Cheever comes in and asks questions I can't answer. I have to set up the funeral. To top it off, Jim's parents blame me for his death."

Heather arched a thinly plucked brow. "Why blame you?"

"Who knows? It may be they're distraught and no one else is convenient."

"You don't suppose the killer will come after you, do you?"

"It sure has crossed my mind. I guess it depends on whether he found what he was looking for. I wish I knew what it was. I'd gladly give it up and be done with it."

"You don't have any idea at all?" Heather was whispering.

"None. Nada. The FBI said Jim was working in a firm with mob connections. That's about all I can get them to say. Cheever wants me to search for evidence. Crap!" She chewed on a fingernail. "It would have to be in an envelope with 'evidence' stamped on the front for me to find anything."

"Listen, I'll be glad to help look. I am, after all, on my very last assignment for my PI certificate. I can give you pointers."

Trish looked up at Heather and suppressed a smile. This was perhaps the only friend she had in the world. It might help to have someone at her side. To top it off, she really didn't want to be alone in that house just yet. "Sure, why not?"

The grin on Heather's face threatened to stretch from ear to ear. "Great! Let me know what I can do."

"If all goes as the doctor told me, I should be released sometime tomorrow afternoon. I'll give you a call and you can pick me up."

"I'll probably have to work 'til five, but I'll shoot on over when I get off. Where do we start?"

"The only place I haven't thoroughly searched myself. The house."

****

Heather picked up Trish in her new Mustang and they literally raced to the Tudor. Relieved she had arrived in one piece, Trish motioned for Heather to pull around to the back of the house.

Hmm, I guess it's all mine, now. One thing I know,

I'm going to get rid of it as soon as I can. Too many memories and bad experiences. Oh, Jim, why couldn't we have lived happily ever after? What changed you? Was it me? She shook her head. *Not the time to feel sorry for myself. The sooner I find what Cheever's looking for, the sooner he'll leave and I can start my life over.* She headed up the sidewalk, resolving to tackle the sale of the house soon.

With the advent of fall, the house was dark, even at 6 p.m. Spiraling leaves blew across the driveway. Trish shivered in the chill of the evening as she unlocked the kitchen door. She noted thankfully the shattered glass had been cleaned up and a piece of plywood fitted to replace the broken pane.

Trish flipped on the lights. Heather practically bounced inside and began opening cabinets.

"No. We don't need to look there. The Feds have gone over the house inch by inch. If something is here, it would be inconspicuous. Only I have no idea what or where. I'd guess it would be in a spot I don't see very often. Some cubbyhole or back of a closet. You take the den and I'll take Jim's office."

"Got it. Boy, this is fun. My first case. We're looking for something containing evidence, right?"

"Yes. It's all a riddle to me. How do you find something when you don't know what you're looking for?"

"They told me in PI school to look for the obvious. That's the thing everyone misses."

"Yeah, whatever that means."

For the next two hours, they examined every room in the house. Nothing even resembling evidence was found. Heather entered the office and tapped Trish on the shoulder.

She jumped. "Oh crap, you scared me."

"Sorry. This isn't getting us anywhere. I'm beat." She plopped down in the only easy chair still usable. Stuffing flew up from the ripped cushion.

Trish nodded and sat on the floor. "Here, here. I'm all searched out. I'm beginning to think we'll never find anything." Her cell phone rang; Trish crawled on the carpet and pulled her purse from the desk. "Hello?"

"So, did you find the stuff yet?"

Mixed emotion flooded her mind. It was him. That man was like a giant hornet, buzzing in her ear. But, it would be best not to upset a murderer.

"What stuff? I have no idea what I'm looking for. Why don't you just leave me alone?"

"Now, where would be the fun in that? What we need is computer files. Records and receipts. Look for lists of numbers. You know your husband. Think where he would hide them."

"Did you kill him?" *Sure, blurt it out and make him mad.*

A pause. "Nothing personal. Just a job." Somehow the soft voice didn't match the image she had of him.

Trish couldn't stop herself. She had to know why. "Do you have no feelings? Are you an animal?"

"I've been called that. It probably applies. When that's what you've been trained to do, it's hard to find a nice cushy job with those qualifications."

"I think you're sick."

"Can't argue. I'll be calling." The phone went dead.

Heather pulled on Trish's arm. "What was that all about? Was it him?"

"Yes. He told me we should look for records and receipts, lists of numbers. Whatever that means."

Heather ran her hands over the keyboard on a pullout shelf under the desk. "Did you look in the computer?"

"The FBI took it and his laptop. They've found nothing so far."

"Then we have to find a disk or flash drive. Did you have a safe deposit box?"

"Feds are looking at that as well. I'm inclined to agree with you that a disk or flash is where we'll find what we're looking for. But where?"

"Tell me about Jim's work habits." Heather threw her right arm across her belly, then rested her left elbow on her right hand. She chewed on her left thumbnail and leaned back in her chair.

"That's just it. I don't know what they were. I was banned from the office. The only thing I ever did was deliver glasses of iced tea. He'd drink four or five in a three-hour period."

"Iced tea? You brought it to him?"

"Yes, so?"

Heather pointed to the desk. "Then why did he need a thermos?"

"For water, I suppose…"

They both reached for the jug at the same time.

Heather held the jug and grinned at Trish. "My idea. Let me look, please."

Trish grabbed the thermos as well. "It's Jim's, let me have it." As she jerked it out of Heather's hand, they each lost their grip. The silver container banged onto the floor. Shattered glass could be heard as it rolled on the carpet. "Look what you've done."

"Don't blame me. I didn't yank it out of my hand."

"I'm sorry. I guess I'm still jumpy. It's a little creepy being in this house again. This whole thing is pissing me off."

"Just don't take it out on me. I'm trying to help."

"I know, Heather. My bad." Trish picked up the thermos. She shook it. "Something definitely broke."

"Duh, probably the glass bottle inside. Let's take it to the kitchen and dump it out."

They hurried to the kitchen holding the container as if it were fragile. Trish unscrewed the cap and looked inside. "Looks like water." She dumped the contents into the sink. Water spewed out and nothing else. She looked inside and shook her head. "Nothing there."

Heather grabbed the jug and shook it next to her ear. "Sounds like something else inside besides glass. Metal, I'd say. I've broken a few of these myself. The insides can be replaced from the bottom." She twisted the plastic cap while holding it over the counter.

"Just a minute. I don't want tiny pieces of glass all over the sink." Trish unrolled some paper towel and smoothed it out on the counter.

Heather bent over the towel and turned the bottom of the thermos. She peered inside. "Don't see anything." She turned the jug upside down and gently pulled on the rim of the glass. Shards fell out.

"There. Look at that." Trish pointed to what appeared to be a baggie wrapped in a rubber band and taped to a large jagged piece of glass. She picked it up, carefully peeling back the tape, unwrapped the package, and emptied the contents.

Two silver flash drives lay like high-tech Pick-Up-Stix, one on top of the other.

Chapter Twenty-Six

Heather caught her breath and reached for the flash drives.

Trish blocked her arm. "No, don't touch them. What about fingerprints?"

Trish's friend scooped up the drives and headed out of the kitchen. "Silly, the fingerprints will be Jim's. We need to look at this stuff."

"Where are you going?"

"To my place. I have a computer."

"Wait for me."

They hurried to Heather's car. Trish barely had time to get her seat belt fastened before they were lurching to a stop in front of Heather's three-story apartment building. Old-fashioned streetlights, tall bushy oak trees, and Victorian homes lined the quiet avenue.

The women took the stairs two at a time pausing only long enough to unlock the imposing front door. Once inside the four-room apartment, Trish tried to slow her breathing by using controlled breathing. "Didn't realize you were trying to kill me, too."

Heather pulled back the drapes and peered outside. "Never know who's watching. Got a murderer out there, not to mention the Feds." She slipped to the other side of the window and looked out once more. "I think the coast is clear."

"Sheesh. Sounds like a bad episode of a 'Days of Our Lives' soap. Sorry, that was redundant."

Heather dropped the curtain in place and made sure the edges were tight together. "Hey, I happen to like that show. Don't get to see it except on the late-night rerun. Anyway, let's go take a look at our evidence."

Trish followed her friend down a hall toward the den. The walls of the hall were decorated with framed 8x10 photographs of flowers, landscapes, and outdoor shots. She stopped in front of a two-tone pink rose in full bloom. "Heather, did you do these?"

"Yeah, my other hobby. Remember that art show I exhibited in last month? I sold four of my pictures that day."

"They're gorgeous. You have a real talent. I knew you took a lot of snapshots, but I had no idea you were this good. They weren't up when I was here last. How long has it been? A month? I'm impressed."

Heather did a low bow. "Why, thank you, ma'am. I guess I am pretty good."

They entered a small room containing an easy chair, two bookshelves filled to overflowing, and a desk, complete with a computer and keyboard on a shelf underneath. Heather took one of the flash drives and leaned over the computer. She inserted it into the back and sat in the leather swivel chair.

"Here we go." The screen flickered; seconds of black screen with an hourglass in the middle transformed into a box stating "J. Morgan, broker — File Pirate 1 — Password _____ "

"Crap. What's his password?" Heather's hand poised over the keyboard.

Trish looked at Heather with a blank stare. "I have

no idea. Like I told you, this office was off limits. I wasn't even allowed to dust it."

They tried birthdates, mother's maiden name, favorite color, first car. Nothing worked. The second drive opened the same way, needing a password.

Trish plopped into the easy chair. "We're stuck. I've run out of ideas. I tried to think if he had a pet he told me about. Nothing hit me."

"We can't give up. What about old girlfriends, or places he loved to visit?"

"We never went on vacations. He thought they were a waste of time. If you love your work, why go somewhere and miss out?"

"Wow, I feel for you, girl. For six years, you never went anywhere?"

"He did, on business, but not me. He said I'd be bored to tears and he didn't want me to endure that."

"He didn't have any other interests at all?"

"He enjoyed opera, and as a young man, was a very good tennis player. Promising, even, until a knee injury sidelined his dream."

"Any famous relatives or acquaintances?"

"He met some Hollywood people on one of his trips, but no one he was impressed with. Thought they were all show and no substance."

"Got to think harder. Anything, no matter how insignificant." Heather stood up and stretched. "I need a drink. How 'bout you? Got some beer or wine."

"Maybe some ice water. If I have anything stronger, I'll probably slide under the table and nap for six hours."

"One ice water comin' up. Want some lemon?"

"Great, thanks."

Heather walked into the hall and hollered over her shoulder. "You try to think of something else to try while I'm gone."

Trish got up and sat at the desk staring at the screen. *What would you use, Jim? My name?* Her fingers touched the keys. *Nope. What else?* Something Heather said suddenly triggered a memory. *Famous relative.* Jim had discovered he was a distant relative of Henry Morgan, the pirate. He had been intrigued and had done some research on the buccaneer. He became an expert on the man's history.

On the screen it said, File name Pirate 1. No, it couldn't be. She typed in "Henry". Nothing Then she typed "Henry Morgan" and the screen flipped to a flying parrot saying "Avast, ye landlubbers." The parrot disappeared and a listing of files filled the black space.

"Holy shit! I got it. Heather," she yelled.

"You did? Wonderful." She set a glass of water on the side of the desk. Taking a swig of beer, Heather sat and studied the file names. They were a mixture of numbers and letters that made no apparent sense. She double clicked on the first file, another password box appeared.

"Nuts, looks like he had passwords for each file. What was the key that got you in?"

"Henry Morgan."

"Who's that?"

"The pirate. Jim was a relative."

"Ah, I see." Heather thought a minute. "What were pirates always after, besides damsels?"

"Treasure?"

"*Voila*! That works on this file anyway. We need to copy these files to another storage place. I've got a place on the Internet that stores files for you. I'll download them to it. Take a few minutes. Drink your water and leave it to me."

Trish sat back in the easy chair and relaxed. *How good is it to have a friend like this? When this ordeal is over, I'm going to do something special for her. Hopefully, it'll be over soon. Don't see the problem…*

Heather's phone rang interrupting Trish's thoughts.

"Hello, talk to me." Heather listened and inhaled deeply, then glanced sheepishly at Trish as she hit the speaker button. She mouthed, "It's him. The son of a bitch has my number."

Chapter Twenty-Seven

"Did you and your friend find my stuff?"

At the sound of his voice, a bead of sweat rolled down Trish's back.

Heather regained her composure. "No, we haven't. Don't call me anymore."

Trish pictured the sneer on his face as he made a clucking sound with his tongue. "You're not a very good liar. I know you have it 'cause I saw you run out of the Morgan house and zip over to your place."

Damn, he knows where we are. Bastard must be right outside! Trish ran to the window and stood sideways. She grabbed the shade between her thumb and forefinger and looked outside. Carefully replacing the shade she went over to Heather's desk and picked up a sticky note pad. She wrote, "Don't see anyone. There's a Fed car out there."

To the phone Heather said, "All right, we've got it, but it's password protected. You want to try to figure it out yourself?"

Silence then, "You do that. Find the password and let me know. I'll give you one hour. No more." The phone clicked off and a steady annoying buzz replaced the man's voice. Heather slapped the off button.

Trish rubbed her head. The perpetual headache from the past couple of days pounded, frustration surfaced. She was sick of this whole mess. She wanted everything to go away. "Let's just give him what he wants and be done with it."

Heather got into Trish's face. "You think he's going to let us walk up to him, hand him the drives, and then let us go? Are you insane? We're witnesses. And you know what criminals say about witnesses. The only good one is a dead one." The doorbell rang and she jumped. "Crap. Who's that?"

Heather opened the door as Agent Cheever was about to push the bell again. "Hey, Heather. Get any calls lately?" He smiled knowingly.

Heather looked past Cheever. A nervous young man stood behind him, grinning with a plastic, forced smile. She frowned. "You guys tapped my phone, didn't you?"

"Of course. We couldn't take any chances. Um, may I come in?" Cheever didn't wait for an answer. He stepped inside. His companion followed.

Heather swept her hand from shoulder to knee and bowed toward Cheever's back. "Pardon my manners. What would my mama say? Shame on me. Do come in." She slammed the door. "What the hell do you want now?"

"We wondered if you found the code word yet?"

"We're working on it. And we don't need any help, thank you."

Cheever pointed to his partner. "This is Agent Biff Robbins. He's a genius on the computer. He can decipher any password. He'll find it for you."

"Biff? Who would name their kid Biff?" Heather asked.

The man gave a half-hearted smile. "Yeah, I know. Mom wasn't good with names. But I can solve computer problems. Where's the computer?"

Heather stepped in front of the man. "Hold on, Biff. I think we can do it. Do you think the guy you're after would feel comfortable with FBI geeks hogging the keyboard? I suggest you two hightail it out of here and make it obvious so it looks like we are still trying to get the info for him. Otherwise we're dead."

"Oh, no, we're not leaving. We're dealing with a professional killer here. If this is who we think it is he's done at least twelve jobs in the past five years."

Heather jabbed her hands on her hips. "I don't give a rat's behind about anything but saving our butts. We think we have something but if we can't deliver we're goners. Do you want that on your conscience? You need to go look for him. He's in the area right now."

Cheever rubbed his chin. "Maybe you've got a point. Okay. We'll monitor and remain close. I don't like having civilians involved, so be careful. Don't take any chances. Let us handle everything else."

"Yeah, you don't want to get in trouble if we get hurt. Looks bad on your record," Heather said.

Cheever grinned and winked. "That, too. Okay, we're out of here. Come on, Biff."

The Feds left, Heather and Trish retreated to the den. Heather refreshed the computer screen. She typed a few commands and the startup of Spider Solitaire filled the picture.

"Hey, what are you doing?"

"Nothing to do but wait for a call. Might as well get in a game or two. Uh, why don't you make us some coffee? I can't stand mine."

"Heather, sometimes you drive me up the wall."

"Oh, you're just trying to give me a compliment.

Coffee's in the third cabinet to the right, over the sink."

One hour from the first call Trish's ring tone sounded.

"You got it?"

Heather came over and leaned in to hear the conversation. "We got it. What now?"

"I want it and any copies you've made. Don't mess with me. I know you have copies."

Trish held the phone to her chest. "Again, let's just give him what he wants."

Heather whispered. "What happens when we hand him the drives? He's not going to let us go. We've been over this. Wake up, Trish! He wants us dead."

"I can hear what you're saying." That voice burrowed into Trish's head again. "I just want those files back. You won't be harmed. You haven't seen me so why would I kill you? I get paid for a job and this one is only to retrieve information. Now be a good girl and tell me what it is. A disk or a drive?"

A glimmer of a plan took shape in Trish's head. Why not give him only one drive and hold onto the other? Then they could turn it over to the cops, who could use it to catch this guy.

"It's a disk drive. One of those flash things." Trish noticed Heather had returned to her computer and was typing on the keyboard.

"Here's what you do. Take it to the post office and put it in box one oh five. The door will be open. You won't be harmed." He chuckled. "We can part friends."

"Friends, my ass. Let's just get it done."

The voice's tone stiffened noticeably. "I know the Feds have been there. They left a man outside. You'll have to ditch him. Be there in ten minutes." The phone went dead. Trish glanced at the clock on the kitchen wall. Just after 9:30.

Heather reached behind her computer and pulled out a flash drive. She sat at her desk and worked for a couple of minutes with her back to Trish. Then she got up, walked over, and asked, "So what did the guy say?"

"We're to leave the flash drives at the post office. I'm leaving just one and not telling him about the other one."

"Don't worry about it." Heather held up two gold chains. Dangling from each were three black flash drives. "I made copies of both."

Chapter Twenty-Eight

The Millvale post office occupied a downtown corner lot with three parking spaces for customers. Trish finally convinced Heather that only one of them needed to make the delivery. Heather wanted to go fully armed, but Trish explained the FBI might shoot her in the confusion.

The post office was only four minutes from Heather's apartment. The grizzled postmaster stopped sweeping the floor behind the counter when Trish entered. He looked at her over half glasses perched on the end of a bulbous nose. "What can I do fer ya, Mrs. Morgan?"

"Nothing, thanks. I'm just going to the mail slots."

"Shucks, haven't had a customer for at least two hours. I'm afraid I'll sweep the last of this old linoleum away if someone doesn't come in." He held the broom upright in front of him with both hands and grinned. "When nobody's here, me and Mrs. Broomster do some dancin'." He did a pirouette around the broom and chuckled.

"You make a charming couple, Mr. Warren." Trish forced a grin and checked her watch. Only two minutes to find the box in question. She waved at the old man and hurried around the corner to the bank of mailboxes.

As she was told, it was empty and open. She glanced around. The hallway was small and well lit and she was alone. Trish placed four flash drives in the box and closed the door. She wanted to run all the way back to Heather's, but she mustered up the strength to walk back, albeit quickly.

Well, let's hope that is over with. Maybe I can begin to put my life back together. Oh, my gosh, I haven't called Jim's mom about the funeral arrangements. She'll be furious at having to make plans at the last minute.

Trish was just disconnecting from alerting her mother-in-law that the funeral was two days away when she approached Heather's place. She pushed open the door and heard a groan.

"Heather?" The living room was empty. She thought she heard Heather moving around in another part of the apartment. *I hope I'm not interrupting her and Max.* "You there?" She tiptoed down the hall toward Heather's bedroom.

As she opened the door, she was grabbed around the neck and thrown into the bedroom. She stumbled onto the bed and rolled into Heather. Heather's hands were tied, her mouth was duct-taped. Her eyes were wild and full of fire.

Trish flipped around and stared into a pistol.

To her astonishment, the face behind the gun was familiar.

"Mr. Davis?" She asked in disbelief.

He was still in his mailman uniform, but the gun was not standard mailman issue. "Yep. It's me. I'm sorry for this mess, Mrs. Morgan. My cover is blown anyway, so I have to move again. A handicap in my line of work."

"You're the killer?"

He laughed. "I prefer *professional hit man*. Sounds more civilized, don't you think?"

"No, I don't think." Trish moved to the end of the bed.

Davis wiggled the pistol at her. "Uh-uh. Stay right there. I'm afraid I must truss you up just like your friend. Turn over please and put your hands behind your back."

"What do you intend to do with us? You aren't going to get away. The FBI is here. If you shoot, they'll hear."

Davis sidled up next to the window and eased the shade open. "Huh, just like I thought. The Fed left when he saw you go the post office. I just need to get my information and I'll be going. Now do as I say. Turn over."

Ten minutes later, Trish lay beside Heather on the bed with hands and feet bound.

Davis hurried off to the living room. Trish heard him working the keyboard. She jiggled and with effort turned to face Heather.

Once again she flipped over and scooted to the top of the bed. She wriggled and was able to get a grip on the tape over Heather's mouth with her shackled hands. Pulling hard, she lost her grip. But with three more attempts, it was off.

Heather spat and inhaled deeply. "Where's my gun?" she hissed. "I'm gonna blast that sucker to smithereens."

Trish wildly shook her body, trying to draw Heather's attention toward her gag. Finally, the message got through and she was again breathing normally.

"Quiet," she whispered. "Can you get my hands?"

"I think so."

"Not a good idea, ladies."

At the sound of Davis's voice Trish wanted to cry. But she wouldn't give him the satisfaction. "That tape won't come off so easy." He lifted each woman up to a sitting position. "Now, I'm going to remove the tape from your feet so you can walk. Please pay attention. If you want to stay alive, you'll do as I say. No questions. I'm not a patient man. Agreed?"

Both women nodded.

He pulled a large knife from his pants and cut the tape holding their legs. Blood rushed back to her ankles. Spikes of pain shot through as the circulation restarted. *God, please don't let him kill us. This can't be happening. The mailman, for heaven's sake.*

Davis stood up and stepped back. "You ladies are my insurance in case my plan falls short. Believe me you're in good hands." He laughed loudly. "I like that. You're in good hands. Insurance." Davis slapped his knee. "Sometimes I'm hilarious. Okay, here's what we're going to do. I have a limo waiting. Actually, it really is a limo. I borrowed it so we could have some privacy."

Heather cleared her throat. "You are insane. You don't know you're just minutes from death, do you?"

"Who's doing the dirty deed?"

"The Feds are not far from here. They know where we are. Got news for you, bud, the Cavalry's on its way."

"Now that's funny. They haven't a clue. Anyway, we'll be out of here in minutes." He held up his hand. The other four drives swayed from gold chains. "I got

146

what I came for. Oh, by the way, Heather. That file you made for the FBI—I erased it. Nice try. So, shall we go?"

Davis looked left and right and directed them out the side door and down the steps. As he'd said, a black limo sat in the alley behind the building next door. He pointed to the car. "Hurry up." He herded them to the rear door; they awkwardly climbed inside. Closing the door, he got into the driver's seat and tucked his mop of red hair under a chauffeur's cap. He touched the top of the hat. "Makes it official. Enjoy the ride."

He steered the limo onto the street and inserted a Metallica CD into the player. He turned up the sound so loud Trish's ears hurt. She unsuccessfully tried to move her hands into a more comfortable position. Her arms ached from being tied behind her. Heather looked stunned as well as mad. *That's a duh. Me, too.* She peered out of the tinted windows and was shocked to see they were driving right past the post office.

Cheever sat in an unmarked car with a phone to his left ear, his other hand covering the right ear. He looked annoyed as the noisy limo inched past. Several agents paced in front of Cheever's car. The postmaster stood outside the door, looking amused at the commotion. The federal agent, however, was not amused and was yelling into the phone. Bob Jenkins stood off to one side, with arms crossed and a frown on his face. The men disappeared from sight. Trish wondered if she'd ever see Bob again. For that matter, would she ever see anyone again?

Chapter Twenty-Nine

Trish's childhood fantasy of her first limo ride had included a bouquet and front-row concert tickets. Yet here she sat trussed up like a Thanksgiving turkey, struggling to stay upright with hands uncomfortably duct-taped behind her back. Heather no longer muttered curses at Davis. She had settled into the corner of the back seat and was forcing her hands in front by scrunching up and pulling them under her long legs. Heather inched them up to her calves. Her head now rested on her knees. Her breath came in short bursts. "Shit! I can't get them any farther. I think I wrenched my back. I'm going to beat the snot out of that sucker when I get free."

Trish couldn't imagine how she was going to do that. For that matter, how were they going to get out of this alive?

They sped through residential Millvale and onto blacktopped roads, passing into a less inhabited area. After they crossed a one-lane bridge that spanned a nearly dry creek, the road became lined with a heavy stand of trees blocking most of the sun. The limo suddenly swerved onto a faint path through the forest. They lurched among trees that sometimes scraped the sides of the vehicle. Davis guided the car deeper into the forest, making several turns. Trish guessed they had gone at least a mile and a half when they pulled up beside an old trailer.

It rested in a clearing so thoroughly surrounded by trees that Trish couldn't spot the opening they had just come through. In fact, she had no idea such a large wooded patch existed this close to town. Crows announced their dissatisfaction with a human presence. Rays of light filtered through the trees. In any other situation, this would have been a great spot for a picnic.

An older model, green-camouflaged pickup sat in back of the metal-domed trailer. Davis parked the limo off to one side and climbed out. "Here we are, ladies. Home sweet home." He opened the car door and laughed, an ugly derisive sound. "Well, Heather, you got yourself in a tizzy, didn't you?"

He dug in his pocket, found a pocketknife, and slit the tape holding her hands. She expelled a breath, stretched her legs, and rose to a sitting position. "I don't think I could have lasted another minute bent over like that." She arched her back and twisted her neck. Davis produced a roll of tape and rebound Heather's hands behind her.

"Time to get out, girls." Davis took Heather's arm and pulled her out of the limo. She almost fell as she tried to gain her balance. "Don't you think you ought to just get out of here? The cops won't be far behind." Trish leaned against the limo to get her balance.

"I think the cops have no idea where I'm at. Cheever is as dumb as a bag of donuts. Besides, it's time to move on. I'm just going to grab my gear and be off. You just sit by that tree and relax. Take me a few minutes."

Davis locked the limo door and sauntered over to the trailer. He took a last look at the women and disappeared inside. Heather squirmed closer to Trish. "Get your hands over here so you can get in my sock."

Trish arched one brow. "What?"

"Come over here. I got a Swiss Army knife in my sock."

Trish looked at the white cotton socks Heather wore. "You're putting me on, right?"

Heather gritted her teeth. "No, I got it in my PI kit. Get over here. The sock on my right foot. We can get him."

"You're nuts. We're here alone with a killer—a professional killer. You'll only piss him off. Not me, sister. Let's just go."

"Do you think he's just going to hop in his redneck truck and motor off into the sunset? He's not leaving two witnesses to identify him. Use your brain. Now, get the knife. Hurry."

Trish's anger surfaced but she had to admit Heather had a point. "Okay, let's get the hell out of here."

"Not yet."

Trish looked up at her friend. "What do you mean, not yet?"

Heather smiled demurely. "We're going to catch a killer."

"The hell we are. Use your brain. We're both amateurs here. I never was good in a fight. I cry when I break a nail, for God's sake."

"Hey, it's two against one and we have surprise on our side."

"Pardon me, Heather, but with you talking like this the only thing we have on our side is stupidity. I'm not going to get the knife if you keep insisting on getting us killed."

"We have this one chance to save our lives," Heather sputtered. "Get the stinking knife. I'll keep watch for Davis."

Reluctantly, Trish shimmied over to Heather's feet. She was about to reach for the sock.

"Stop!" Trish froze. Heather rolled her eyes toward the trailer. The door had swung open. Davis appeared carrying a duffle bag and two rifles tucked under his arm. He glanced at them and hurried around to his truck. They heard him stow his stuff in the bed and watched him return inside the trailer.

"Hurry."

Trish fumbled with the hem of the sock and finally was able to reach inside. She grabbed the knife and pulled it out. "Now what?"

"The second tool on the knife is a pair of scissors. See if you can open it."

Trish moved back to a position next to Heather. "No, not that one. The next one. There. Pull it out. Good, you've got it. I'll put my hands over there and you cut the tape."

Davis came out of the truck two more times before Trish cut through the tape.

Then Trish's hands were free.

Heather rubbed her hands. "Okay, here's what we'll do. After he goes in the next time, we race to the door. It swings out so we stand to the left side. When he comes out, we slam the door into him. Got it?"

"That won't work. He'll just be shoved back into the trailer where he has guns. We're dead."

"I guess you're right. We need a weapon. Look around."

Trish spotted a woodpile behind the truck. "Hey. I'll bet there's a log over by that wood. See it? Behind the truck."

"Yeah, that should do it. Let me swing the thing. I was All State in softball for two years running. A four fifty-five average for my career."

"Heather, you are a raving lunatic but I guess I'm ready."

Davis slammed the door open again and hauled another load to the back of his truck. Trish and Heather sat still and tried to look innocent. Trish just knew Davis would see their plan written all over their faces. Or worse yet, that he would come over and check on their restraints. But, he gave them a quick look and disappeared once more.

They scrambled to their feet and raced to the woodpile. Heather picked up a three-foot, bat-sized log and swung it. She winked at Trish. "Perfect. Heavy enough to do some damage. Let's roll."

They huddled just outside of the mark on the side of the trailer where the door would hit. Heather held the bat like a player ready for a fastball. They waited. It seemed like hours before the door flew open. Trish heard a whoosh. Heather's weapon thonked off Davis's head; he collapsed.

Heather stepped around Davis' inert body and started for the truck. Trish kneeled beside him and began going through the man's pockets.

Heather stopped and turned. "Come on," she yelled. "Let's go. What the hell are you doing?"

"Looking for the duct tape. I'm going to truss him up."

"Forget it. Find some keys and come on."

"Damn, I can't find the tape."

"Screw the tape! Get the keys."

"They're not here either. No keys at all. I saw Davis lock the Limo so check the truck and see if the keys are there."

Trish sprinted to the truck. The ignition was bare. "Lord, where are they?" She looked back at Heather who was racing to the Limo. *What is she doing? We need to go.* Then she smiled as her friend stabbed every one of the Limo's tires.

Heather ran up to the truck. "Did you get them?"

"They're not here."

"Did you look in the visor? Here, let me. Crap, they aren't here."

Trish swallowed to try to get her heart in its proper place. "Now what, smarty? What if he comes to? He's not going to be happy."

Heather waved to the other side of the truck. "Don't worry about it. Get in the truck."

"So, we're just going to sit here and wait for help?"

"What else do you suggest? Our cell phones are back at the house and we're so far out in the boonies I doubt yelling would get anyone's attention. So, get in and shut up. I can hot wire it and get us out of here. Let me do it."

Trish climbed into the passenger side, sweeping fast food wrappers off the seat.

Heather felt under the dash and pulled out some wires. She used her Swiss Army knife to strip the insulation and twisted two wires together. The truck started up and she threw it into gear. The wheels spun and finally caught. The pickup lurched around the trailer. They raced past their kidnapper and headed through the forest.

"Do you know the way out?"

"I sure hope so." Heather headed the truck through the trees. They bounced and jiggled on the bench seat as the truck bumped over ruts and tree roots. Heather wrestled the truck between and around obstacles. They made countless turns and backtracks. Several minutes later, Heather jammed on the brakes.

Trish hit her head on the dash and came up sputtering. "Why did you stop?"

Heather pointed. "Take a look."

Trish rubbed away the pain from her forehead and stared open-mouthed. There, about a hundred yards in front of them, was that damn trailer.

Davis was nowhere to be seen.

"Damn," Heather muttered. "I knew I should have busted his kneecaps after I conked him on the head."

Chapter Thirty

"God, what do we do now?" Heather sighed. "Where's Davis?"

Trish tried to ignore the flock of humming birds fluttering inside her stomach. "I see that. If he's conscious, he had to hear his stupid truck. Probably inside tending to his headache. We need to grab his guns."

Heather nodded. "Right, you take a pistol and I'll use a rifle."

Trish shook her head. "I want the rifle. I'm a better shot with it."

"I thought you didn't like guns."

"I don't, but I never said I don't know how to shoot. My dad was a hunter who insisted his little girl learn about firearms."

Trish opened the door and cringed when it squeaked, echoing through the woods. She didn't latch the door behind her, trying to keep down the noise. Heather followed and they rummaged through the bed of the truck, finding two rifles, several boxes of shells, and a pistol.

Trish grabbed a rifle. Heather chose the revolver. They loaded their weapons and hunched down beside the pickup, waiting for Davis to show himself.

The birds began to jabber again after being disturbed by the women at the truck. The sun settled behind the thicket of trees. It was turning colder. Trembling, Trish wondered if she could possibly shoot someone. A deer or rabbit was hard enough, but a human? Even a dirt bag like Davis would be a challenge she wasn't sure she wanted to face.

They leaned on the Ford's fender and watched. The only sound, other than the birds, was the wind fluttering through the remaining fall leaves.

When the bullet hit the front of the truck inches from Heather's head, they both screamed. Heather fell backward and, for a second, Trish thought she'd been shot. A quick glance proved otherwise. Trish's legs were so cramped she could not stand up. That proved to be a good thing because another bullet ricocheted off the truck's window post close to the top of her head.

Heather scrambled to a kneeling position and aimed her pistol at the trailer. "Wait, Heather. Don't waste any bullets. Did you see where the shots came from?"

"No."

"I didn't either, but it sounded like they came from near the woodpile. Do you see him?"

"No. Just let me drill that sucker. He scared the shit out of me."

"Me, too."

"There. I saw some movement. You were right. That's where he is."

Trish took aim. She put four rounds into the logs; five of the pieces of wood rolled onto the ground. Then it was quiet again.

Davis yelled from behind the woodpile. "Well, ladies, I see you've fired a rifle before. Looks like a Mexican standoff. How about we call a truce?"

Trish put four more bullets into the wood. Heather emptied her pistol as well. Trish yelled as loudly as her dry throat would allow, "Throw down your rifle and come out with your hands up." *Never thought I'd ever say that.*

Much cursing and muttering came from Davis' position.

Trish yelled again. "Do it now or that wood becomes splinters."

Heather held a pistol with both hands. "Better do as she says, sucker. I'm pretty impressed with her accuracy."

"All right. Hold your fire. I'm coming out."

Trish kept her position. "Throw out all your weapons. Whatever you've got."

A rifle helicoptered out and landed on the ground between them and Davis. Then a knife landed close to it. "That's all I got."

"Come on out."

Davis rose from behind the woodpile. He had a large white bandage around his head and still wore his uniform. He stepped in front of the wood and began moving toward them. He had a smile on his face.

"That's far enough. Lie face down on the ground. Do it now." Trish hoped she sounded like she meant it.

Davis just stood there. "Have either of you ever killed someone? It's not pretty. Death is very ugly. You must live with that all your life." He moved forward again.

Trish shouted. "Stop. I'll shoot."

Davis' smile never wavered. He took one more step—only about twenty yards away.

Trish didn't hear the shot and didn't remember

pulling the trigger. Davis went down, grabbing his foot. "You bitch. You shot me."

"Yes, I guess I did. I'll do it again. The plus is I won't have to field dress you. That always makes me queasy. Now lie flat on the ground. Heather, get something to tie him up." Trish kept the rifle trained on the man as he rolled around holding his foot, cursing. She decided not to insist upon him lying flat, guessing he wouldn't be jumping up to rush them any time soon.

Heather returned with some electrical cord. She pushed Davis down and bound his hands behind his back, then secured his uninjured leg as well. When she seemed satisfied he couldn't get up, she pulled off his shoe to inspect the damage to his unbound foot.

"Clean through and out the other side. I'll get something to bandage it." She looked up at Trish. "I never figured you'd actually do it. Wow, that was awesome. What a shot."

Trish lowered her rifle and set the safety. "Actually, I was aiming for the ground near his foot."

Heather let out a cackle. "Well, it sure worked. I'll be back as soon as I find some bandages and something we can pour on the wound to make it really sting." She hurried off to the trailer.

Davis moaned and rolled his head sideways to look at Trish. "So what now?"

"Well, that's one thing you don't have to worry about. Relax. And I think it would be best if you don't talk. I'm still mad." Trish rested the rifle on her shoulder and sauntered toward the trailer.

Chapter Thirty-One

Trish found all she needed to tend to Davis's wound in his trailer. The bullet had smashed his instep badly. Some broken bones would need attention when they got back to civilization.

She knelt beside him. Davis winced the whole time she cared for his wound. She remembered her grandmother's admonition about being careful helping stray animals, how they might bite in their pain. Well, she couldn't just let Davis bleed to death. She began to remove his sock.

"Ow. Go easy there, lady. You messed me up bad."

"I suppose there was no reason to shoot you. I think you'd be thanking your lucky stars I didn't blow your kneecap off. And that I am kind enough to give you first aid." Trish gave an extra pull on the knot she had tied. "Are you denying you were going to kill us?"

Davis paused and smiled through a grimace. "Okay, you got me there. But someone in my profession can't afford to leave people around who can testify against him, can he?"

"Don't give me the *profession* BS. You're a piece of crap who sneaks up on innocent victims."

Davis sat up awkwardly, his hands tied behind him. "Not one person I ever eliminated was innocent. I'm very careful about my targets."

Trish waved her hand at him. "What about us?"

She pointed to Heather. "We're innocent. You were going to send us to the great beyond. I don't want to hear any more. You're a cold-blooded killer. Nothing more, nothing less."

Trish got up and headed to the trailer to find out what Heather was doing. Maybe finding a phone or some directions to get them out of here. The beauty of the setting sun was in marked contrast to their circumstances. If she were an artist, the orange and purple reflections on the clouds would be a great inspiration to paint a picture.

How odd. The birds have quit chirping.

"This is the FBI. Throw down your weapons and come out with your hands on your head."

The megaphone's hollow message didn't register at first. Trish stood transfixed. The message was repeated. She blinked, dropped the rifle, and slowly placed her hands on her head.

Heather slammed open the trailer door and stood with her hands on her hips. "Where the hell you been, Cheever? You're about three hours late."

The megaphone barked again. "Hands on your head. Come forward slowly."

Suddenly, a team of men in black ninja outfits carrying weapons, pointed in their direction, surrounded them. Two men hurried over to where Davis lay, two others gently patted Trish and Heather down and told them to sit. Cheever, followed by Bob Jenkins, appeared from behind a tree.

Two minutes later, a man ran up to Cheever and whispered in his ear. He nodded and offered his hand to Heather. "You can get up now, ladies. The area is clear."

Heather ignored his gesture and stood, brushing off her clothes. "Area was clear before you got here."

Cheever acted like he didn't hear her.

Bob helped Trish up. "How'd you know where we were?"

Cheever smiled and interrupted. "GPS from a tracking device we added to the disk. We'd have been here sooner, but this area isn't fully pinpointed yet. What happened? How'd you get away from him?"

Bob Jenkins shot Cheever a harsh look. "Let's find out if they're all right first." He turned to Trish and put his hand on her shoulder. "Are you okay?"

Trish looked into Bob's eyes. Steely concern stared back at her. She had the urge to pat his hand, but held back. "I'm fine, thanks. Just anxious to get home and away from that creep."

****

Several hours later, at the police station, Trish and Heather finished the paperwork. Their story had been repeated three times and recorded. Bob insisted on staying through the entire process and offered to take Trish home. She accepted.

Trish flopped back in the passenger seat of Bob's Monte Carlo. *It's over. So drained. I feel like I've finished my second marathon. Now for a hot bath and some rest.*

Bob climbed in and started the car. He smiled. "Since I'm a cop it would look really bad if we had an accident and you weren't wearing a seatbelt."

Trish sat up. "Oh, you're right." She snapped the belt in place. "I'm just so relieved Davis is in custody and I can go back to being unknown again."

"Trish, I was really worried about you. Cheever

wouldn't give out any information, and I was detailed to help his men get to where they were going. I felt like a gofer. Crap, I *was* a gofer."

"Cheever has a way of making you want to slap him around, doesn't he?"

Bob chuckled. "My thoughts exactly." He looked over at her. "Anyway, I'm glad this worked out okay. You're a hero…ah…I mean heroine. With everything that happened, losing your husband and then being kidnapped…well, you're one hell of a woman. And I mean that in the nicest way."

"Thanks, Bob."

"If there's anything I can do in the coming days, ask. I'll break down some doors if you want. You name it."

"That means a lot to me. If I need something, I'll call."

Bob grinned, staring straight ahead with hands at ten and two on the steering wheel. They were silent during the short ride to the B&B stairs.

Wonder how I'll get through the next few days. What a nightmare this has been. Jim's murder, finding a serial killer in quiet old Millvale, getting kidnapped by that killer, and now, facing a funeral. I know how Job in the Bible must have felt.

Come on, God. Can't you ease up a bit here?

Chapter Thirty-Two

Trish trudged upstairs with feet seemingly encased in concrete blocks. She waved goodbye to Bob and unlocked the door. It was after 3 a.m., so the decision to skip taking a bath was a no-brainer. Trish dropped her purse on the dresser, kicked off her shoes, and rolled onto the softness of the Inn's featherbed mattress. Closing her eyes, she allowed the silence to envelope her. Until someone banged on the communal door between the apartment and Mrs. W.'s part of the house.

"Trish, are you okay? Open up," Mrs. Williams' troubled voice roused her.

"Yes, I'm all right."

"I've made some tea for you. I have it here."

I guess it's not in the cards for me to get any rest tonight. She looked at her clock. *I mean this morning.* "Just a minute, Bev. I'm coming." Trish rolled out of bed and tripped over her shoes as she stepped onto the floor. She opened the door. Bev Williams grabbed her arm and escorted her to the kitchen. More like herded her to the kitchen. She padded down the hall in her hose.

Bev pulled out a chair and motioned Trish into it. "Tell me what happened. I heard you were kidnapped. Are you okay?"

"Yes. Davis took Heather and me as hostages. He's now in jail."

"You poor dear. How awful. Davis? Henry, the mailman?" Bev's eyes appeared twice their normal size behind her glasses.

The teakettle on the stove began a shrill whistle. Bev jumped up and poured hot water into two cups. She plopped a teabag into each cup and placed them on the table along with a plate of fresh blueberry muffins. Bev pushed the plate toward Trish. Grinning, Bev snagged one for herself and sat down on the edge of her chair, leaning forward. "Let's have it."

Between bites and for the fourth time, Trish related the story. Bev was the best source of information the town gossips had and Trish knew she wouldn't be satisfied until the entire story unfolded. She toyed with the idea of writing up a recap when she was more rested to hand out to people so she wouldn't have to repeat it over and over. Bev seemed stunned as she listened to the tale. However, not so stunned that she couldn't manage two more muffins.

"I hope he gets the death penalty for what he did to my precious finch." She glanced lovingly at the surviving finch. "I'll pull the lever myself. I still can't believe we had a serial killer right here in Millvale." Bev shook her head. "I've lived here all my life and don't remember anyone ever being killed. Well, except for Mr. Dennis back in fifty-nine. He got himself caught in the antique threshing machine he was readying for the county fair." She shivered. "Ugly mess that was."

Trish finished her tea and got up to leave.

Bev smiled at her. "You know, Bob was beside himself with worry about you. He was here three or four times, filling me in when he heard anything." Bev winked. "I think he has a thing for you. Mind you, I know you just lost your husband, but it's something to think about. You couldn't find a better man anywhere. And not just 'cause I'm prejudiced either."

Trish turned to go. "Yes, Bob is a good man. Thanks for the tea, Bev." She grinned. "And for the heads up."

****

The alarm rang at 6:30.

Crap, forgot to shut that thing off last night. Trish rolled over and slapped the snooze button. She closed her eyes but couldn't shut off the activity behind her eyelids. It was like her brain was yelling at her to get up. Well, she did have to finalize the funeral arrangements. *God, I hope I'll be able to get through that ordeal. I can just imagine what kind of a scene Jim's mom will make. Always making a point of telling everyone I wasn't the best catch available for her son. And then there's his dad who never had a kind word for anyone.*

Trish sat up on the side of the bed and stretched. Her muscles refused to cooperate; her body seemed to belong to someone else. Somehow she got herself together and, not wanting to bother Bev, decided to walk two blocks to grab some breakfast.

The cold morning air refreshed her a bit. The soreness dissipated on the way back to her room. Next came the dreaded visit to the funeral home. She was determined to give Jim a proper funeral, but had no idea how to pay for it. She made a mental note to go by the house and try to make some sense of their finances. Jim had been so secretive about everything it would take a while to sort things out.

After the meeting with Gerald Boggs, great-grandson of the founder of Boggs Funeral Emporium, Trish wanted to slap the smarmy jerk. His insincere smile and semi-gentle push toward the most expensive casket and arrangements ticked her off. She couldn't leave fast enough after telling him decidedly that she would take the next-to-cheapest casket and no extras.

Trish returned to her apartment and called Heather to see how she was doing. After hearing a tirade about "waking somebody from the dead," she was convinced Heather was doing fine. Then she called Mr. Sloan to let him know she would not be back to work until later in the week. Surprisingly, he told her to take as much time as she needed.

She was preparing to drop by the house to pick up a few more clothes when the phone rang.

"Mrs. Morgan? I'm glad I finally tracked you down. My name is Todd Boston. I'm one of the owners of your late husband's brokerage firm of Dodge, Kelvin and Simone. Your husband was doing some important work for us, and we need to locate a document he had in his possession." *Todd Boston? I don't remember anyone by that name from Jim's firm.* "I wonder if I might meet you at your home to see if we can locate it. When I met with him last week, he set it aside in his desk to add some final details. I have a deadline I must meet by Friday and that paper is critical. It should only take a minute to retrieve. If it weren't vital, I would never have bothered you at this inopportune time."

"I'm really busy and the house is in a mess. I don't have any idea where anything is." Trish hesitated.

"Please, Mrs. Morgan. My very job is on the line here." The man sounded desperate.

"Well, I suppose we could. I do need to go over some things at the house. Okay, maybe we could meet…" Trish glanced at her watch. "…say around one p.m.?"

"Marvelous. I'll see you at one, then. I'm sorry to inconvenience you. You have my deepest gratitude." The phone clicked.

Just what I need. Another detail to take care of. When this funeral is over, I may sleep for a week.

Chapter Thirty-Three

Bev had been hurt Trish passed up one of her Inn's gourmet breakfasts for a lousy McDonald's sandwich, so she acquiesced when Bev ordered her to sit down and have lunch. When Trish finished eating, she placed calls to Bob Jenkins and Cheever, asking them to phone her. She said she would be at her house and then headed out the door for her meeting with Mr. Boston. She didn't remember anyone named Boston ever visiting the house. She definitely would have remembered, since Boston was where she was born. On the other hand, she hardly knew any of Jim's business associates.

When Trish pulled into her driveway, the cul-de-sac was empty. She checked her watch. Ten 'til one. Good, she was early. She fished out her cell and gave Cheever and Bob another call. Neither answered. *Must be wrapping up their investigation.* She let herself in the front door and took off her coat.

"How nice to see you again, Mrs. Morgan." Marciano, clutching a can of soda in his plump fingers, sat in the living room rocking chair as if he were the man of the house. "This is my partner, Mr. Boston." He motioned to a hulk standing next to him. The curly-haired man had a round face and a surly look. He was a giant, taller than Jim. His suit jacket appeared at least two sizes too small for his arms. "I believe you spoke to him on the phone this morning."

Trish's heart slammed her chest and she dropped her purse. "Mr. Marciano? How did you get in? What are you doing here?" She gasped. Her house was in even worse shape than before. Wall shelves pulled down and drawers in the desk and credenza pulled out and emptied.

Trish started to breathe again. "Just what is this all about?" She edged back toward the door.

"That's a fair question. To explain, your husband worked for us. As a matter of fact, his work was critical." He smiled and took a sip of his drink. "I need to have the records he was keeping of our activity."

"I haven't the foggiest idea what you're talking about."

"Well, you're our only hope. We've searched this house thoroughly, and we haven't found what we're looking for." That was obvious. A twister would have caused less destruction. "So we thought we'd ask if there was anywhere else we could look."

This couldn't be happening. What the hell had Jim been involved in? "Look, I was kept in the dark about Jim's business." Trish opened her palms and let them fall to her sides. "I have no idea where he would have kept any records."

"Oh, I know he was secretive. That's what he was paid to be." He snickered and Boston grunted an agreement. "There must be someplace outside the home. Did he have a hiding place?"

"No. There is nothing I can tell you. I don't know."

"Mrs. Morgan, I'm afraid you know something you may not even be aware of. But we will get it out of you. Mr. Boston is adept at securing information. It's often a painful process. I would hate to have to resort to that.

We're all friends here. Let's talk a bit first."

Trish tried to steady herself even though, inwardly, she was shaking. "I do not appreciate being threatened. You may be able to hurt me, but I still can't help you. Don't you think I'd tell you if I knew? I'd left Jim. I have no reason to be loyal to him."

"In my line of work, I'm afraid, people lie to me quite often. An unpleasant part of the business. Now think. There must be something. Do you have a safe deposit box?"

"Yes. The First National Bank. The police have the contents."

"See, I told you. Did he have another computer he used besides the one in the den? Maybe a laptop?"

Slowly, Trish had been backing toward the front door. She felt the door handle behind her and pulled. The hulk moved incredibly fast. He grabbed her hand and swung her back into the living room.

She stumbled on the carpet and fell heavily, jamming her right arm. She yelped. Boston stood in front and grabbed her by the shoulders. With no effort, he hauled her to her feet and returned to his place beside Marciano. He wore a blank expression on his face as if nothing had happened.

Marciano clicked his teeth. "Now, that wasn't very smart. Boston is extremely good at what he does. If I were you, I wouldn't try that again."

Trish held her wrist and winced. Tears leaked from the corner of her eyes. But she was determined not to show fear.

Her cell phone rang. All three stared at the ringing purse lying on the floor. "I'd better answer it. A lot of people know I'm here."

Marciano nodded. "Just be careful what you say. No funny stuff. You'll regret it."

Trish picked up the purse and fished out the phone. *Thank God. It was Bob Jenkins.* Think, girl, think. What do I say? "Hello, Bob."

"Hi, Trish. Just returning your call. What's up?"

Trish ignored his question. She was thinking fast. "Yes, I got that phone number you wanted. Dr. Cheever, the one who treated my pain?" She recited the number for him.

"What phone number? Dr. Cheever?"

"Sorry, I can't talk now. I've got to go, I have company. Hope you feel better soon. I know that doctor will help you." Trish closed the phone and shrugged. "A friend of mine. He broke his leg and is in a lot of pain."

Marciano smiled. "Good, you did well. Now about that computer."

"We had a laptop. The FBI has it, but there wasn't anything on it. Originally, it was mine. We both used it after we got married. Jim cursed it for being so old and painfully slow. My desktop PC is newer but the FBI searched it as well. Those are the only computers I know about. There were some flash drives but the police have them as well. There's nothing else."

"Everyone makes copies and keeps them separate. How about any secret places? An office somewhere? Maybe a safe he seldom used?"

Trish shook her head, trying to ignore the pain in her hand. "No. No!" She cried. "Don't you understand? I never knew what he did. He had another life I wasn't part of." She was defeated. *God, when will this nightmare end?*

J.D. Webb

Marciano smiled. "Believe it or not, I think you're telling the truth. But I still need to find the information. It could be on a computer disk or flash drive. Something small." He thought for a moment. "Did he have a place where he kept Christmas presents he didn't want you to find?"

"We spent the last two Christmases in his hunting cabin on the lake. He stashed presents there." Trish froze. The realization of what she had said hit her and Marciano at the same time.

He grinned broadly. "See. I told you. You know more than you thought. We must visit your cabin."

"I'm not sure I can find it. Jim always drove. It's back in a forest preserve."

"Oh, we'll find it. Mr. Boston, if you would please make arrangements for our trip. Mrs. Morgan and I shall have a nice cup of coffee, won't we?" He gave her an intimidating look.

Trish narrowed her eyes. "Depends on what shape you and your ape left my kitchen in." She turned and headed to the coffee pot. Marciano heaved himself out of his chair with effort and followed close on her heels.

Lord, I'm near the end of my rope here. I need your help. Please make Bob understand my message.

Chapter Thirty-Four

The bright sun reflected off the highway as the Mercedes ate up the miles. For over an hour, Trish had sat wedged in the back seat next to Marciano. A thin, plastic strap bound Trish's hands in her lap. Boston drove, eyes fixed on the pavement, both hands gripping the steering wheel.

Thoughts of possible escape plans darted into Trish's mind, only to be ruled foolhardy. Overpowering two giants who were practiced criminals was impossible. She had no weapons and limited mobility. She sighed and glanced at Marciano.

"It won't be long now. We are almost at the Wisconsin border. Concentrate on remembering where we turn off." Marciano's suit coat bunched around his substantial belly, giving Trish a glimpse of a gun in a shoulder holster.

If only I could grab that gun.

"I told you, I'm not certain I can find this place." In fact, she knew the road well. Early in their marriage, Jim insisted on her traveling with him to learn about the outdoors. He was an excellent hunter and fisherman. Truthfully, Trish had enjoyed many wonderful meals with the bounty from their hunts. But with their marriage shaky at best, it had been at least two years since her last visit. Jim had gone hunting with business associates and had stopped bringing her along.

They headed to the hunting cabin and Trish's ominous future. *What if they don't find what they're looking for? What if they do*? Trish had no doubt the outcome would be the same. She would die.

How weird. For the second time in two days, she faced death. *This only happens in movies or on TV, doesn't it?* Trish had never been a fan of organized religion, or as she called it, corporate religion. She silently asked for God's help. Then she asked herself, why would He help her?

A few miles ahead was the turnoff, a meandering gravel road. There were no neighbors for miles from the cabin. Her only hope was to try to get away before they reached that road.

"Excuse me. I need to stop for a restroom break." She tried to look desperate. Actually, that was no problem. She was desperate.

Marciano frowned. "How far are we from the cabin?"

"I don't know. I told you I'm not sure about any of this. Unless you want a mess in your nice car, we need to stop soon." Trish shifted in her seat to emphasize the request.

Marciano sighed. "Mr. Boston, when you come to the next exit, let's find a gas station."

Boston nodded.

An exit sign showed a logo for a mini-mart. Boston guided the Mercedes into the turn and pulled into a gas station a short distance from the interstate. Trish's heart sank seeing only one car parked in front of the main building.

Marciano grabbed Trish's arm in a vicious grip. She winced as he pulled her close. "One false move from you and everyone here will end up dead. Do you hear me?"

Trish tried to twist away from the pain in her bicep. The grip was too tight. "Ow. Yes, I hear you. I just want to go to the bathroom."

"Do we need gas, Mr. Boston?"

Boston looked at the gauge. "Probably wouldn't hurt since we don't know how far we're going. I'll get it." Marciano nodded and sliced through the plastic band on her wrists with a lethal looking blade. He pointed the knife at Trish. "Remember what I said. Everyone in that station is depending on you. They're betting their lives." He closed the blade and stuck it back in his pocket.

Trish tugged on her purse and opened the car door.

Marciano grabbed the handle of the purse and jerked it out of Trish's hand. "Might as well leave this here with me. Can't have you making a call, can we?"

"At least let me get a tissue. You may not care if the toilet paper is gone, but it's an issue with me," she said tartly.

Trish extracted a small packet of tissue, got out, and Marciano followed her inside. A tall gangly attendant behind the counter was encouraging an elderly woman to make a decision about lottery tickets. On her way through the narrow snack aisle, Trish peeked out at the car. Boston swiped a credit card at the pump and began to fill the tank. Trish spotted the restroom sign and headed to the woman's door.

Trish darted into the room and locked the door. She checked the stalls. No one else was there. The lone window was dirty and locked tight. Trish tried to open the window, but it wouldn't budge. *Crap! Must be painted shut.*

A note. She needed to leave a note and hope someone would help. Wouldn't do any good to write on the mirror. She had no doubt Boston would be sent to check the restroom.

A knock on the door startled her. "Time to go, Mrs. M." Marciano jiggled the knob.

"I'm coming. Just a minute." She tore off a paper towel and dug in her slacks for the spare tube of Rose Petale lipstick by Lancôme she always carried.

"You've got thirty seconds exactly."

"No problem." She flushed the toilet and pulled a tissue from her packet. She scribbled a phone number under her message. It read: *I'm being abducted. This is no joke. Heading to cabin at Russell. Please call 555-7112. Trisha Morgan.* She replaced her lipstick in her pocket and wadded the tissue into a ball. Trish unlocked the door and hurried past Marciano, walking fast.

"Hold on, Mrs. M." Marciano's voice had risen and the young clerk, still behind the counter, gave him a questioning look.

Trish waited till Marciano caught up to her. He took her arm and guided her to the restroom door. He opened the door and peeked in. Seemingly satisfied, he herded Trish toward the front door through an aisle stacked with cases of beer. Trish transferred the tissue to her free hand and unfolded it as best she could, waving it behind her. She glanced at the boy, gave him her most sorrowful look, and dropped the tissue onto a display of bottles of windshield washer fluid sitting to one side of the front door. Marciano held the door open and she headed to the car, holding her breath that he would not go back inside.

Boston had the rear car door open and Trish slipped inside. Marciano trudged to the other side and slid in. Trish was not sure but she thought she glimpsed the boy retrieving the tissue and returning to the counter. *Please God, let it be so.*

"Mr. Boston, go check the lady's room for anything unusual our friend here might have left for the police."

"The women's room? Me?"

"Yes, you. Go."

Boston muttered curses all the way in and all the way out. "Nothin' there." He got in and slammed the door.

The ride resumed. Marciano bound Trish's wrists again with a plastic wire. "That really hurts. Do I have to be handcuffed? Where am I going to go if I could get away? Am I going to hurl myself out of a car going seventy or eighty miles an hour?"

Marciano smiled. "I just feel better if you have no possibility of escape. Humor me." He shifted in the corner of the back seat and opened his coat. A bag of cheese puffs appeared, and he opened it. Trish raised an eyebrow; he shrugged. "They'll never miss just one bag."

For the next 15 minutes, Marciano crunched cheese puffs, finishing the entire bag. Trish couldn't watch as the man licked every speck of orange residue covering his fingers.

They came to a sign for Lake Hansen.

"I think this might be the turnoff. Take this exit."

A fork in the road showed Lake Hansen left and Stadler right. "Go toward Stadler. I think our road is down that way. Kind of looks familiar." Trish stared out the window as if searching for a landmark. They drove for a few minutes.

Finally, Trish said, "Nope. This isn't it. We need to go back to the Interstate. I don't think we're far enough yet."

"You're sure?" Marciano did not look pleased.

"Hell, no, I'm not sure. I told you I wasn't that familiar with the place. But you wouldn't listen. All I know is it doesn't take this long to get to the gravel road from the highway."

Marciano sighed. "Back to the highway, Boston."

Two more times Trish led them off an exit and then back to the Interstate.

The last time, Marciano exploded. "I believe you're stalling for time, Mrs. Morgan. It will do no good." He whipped out the same knife and flipped open the three-inch blade. He placed the sharp edge against her cheek. She thought she felt blood begin to trickle. "Now, enough delays and detours. Find me that cabin or you will hurt."

Trish swallowed hard. "I'm trying. I really am. It's just that I can't remember which exit to take. I know we're close." Her heart pounded against her chest. She had stalled as long as she could. Thankfully, he put the knife away again. Brushing her hand across her cheek, she was relieved to find no blood.

The exit for their cabin was the next one. "This off-ramp looks familiar."

Marciano stared at her. "It'd better be."

"Yes, I'm sure now."

They veered onto the exit and came to a stop sign.

"Russell Road. This is it. That's what I've been looking for. Turn right and go about a mile and a half.

There's a dirt road heading south. Take that. It'll have a green mailbox on the right side of Russell."

"Go, Mr. Boston."

The car sped down the highway and turned onto a gravel road. The big Mercedes bounced and shimmied on the uneven surface. Overgrown weeds snatched at both sides of the car. Trees stood as silent sentinels crowding the area. They soon came to a rusted chain link gate blocking the lane. A large silver padlock reflected sunlight in the center of the gate.

"Get us in there, Boston."

The driver slid out of the car. He reached into his jacket pocket and pulled out a black pouch. From it, he extracted a needle-like object. He inspected the padlock and inserted the tool. A little wiggle and the latch popped open. Boston smiled, pulled open the gate, and got back into the car.

Trish looked at Marciano. "I guess you won't be needing a key to the cabin."

Marciano gave her a smirk and shook his head. "How much farther is it?"

"As I remember, we'll come to a curve to the right. The cabin is just beyond. You can pull around back; the dirt track will bring you to the rear of the cabin."

The cabin, constructed of rough-hewn logs, sat on a slight bluff overlooking a fast-running creek. Across the road, a higher bluff faced the cabin, providing a view from the front window of a sheer wall. The track dipped down to a rear entrance in the lower level of the cabin. A crudely built dock led to the water's edge.

Marciano pulled Trish out with him and looked around.

The rear of the two-story log cabin faced the Des

Plaines River. A small, covered landing framed the entrance. A red light on the security system box beside the door blinked at them.

Maciano took a deep breath. "Very nice. I could use a place like this."

Trish grunted. "I wouldn't have guessed you for the outdoors type."

"Don't let my girth fool you. I'm a pretty good hunter. Let's go inside."

It only took a few seconds for Boston to snip the wires and jimmy the door.

The main room was decorated in Southwestern-style furnishings, with chairs made of deer antlers. A huge fireplace, framed in lava rock, filled one side of the room.

"Yes, I could really get used to this place. Mr. Boston, why don't you have a look around? We'll get the fire going and scare up something to eat." He waved his hand at the fireplace. "Mrs. Morgan, will you please?"

Boston left, and Trish loaded three logs from a wood bucket into the fireplace. She soon had a roaring fire.

Marciano motioned Trish into a chair, and then sank into a beige leather couch covered with a colorful Indian blanket. "Now tell me the layout here."

"There are six rooms and two baths. This is the family room. Down the hall is a combined kitchen and dining room, a bath on the left, and a den on the right. Upstairs is a master bedroom with a bath, and two guest rooms."

"I noticed in the front of the house there is only one window on the first floor and none on the second."

"The builders suggested that since the only nice view is in the back we didn't need to waste money on front windows. They just installed one in the family room."

"Good. Where are the weapons?"

"Weapons?"

"Guns, rifles. You said Jim was a hunter. He had to have guns in the cabin. Where are they?"

"Oh, yes. There's a gun case in the den. That's where he keeps some of his hunting rifles and ammunition. His best are kept at home."

Just then Boston entered the room, as if on cue, carrying three rifles and a pistol. "Found these in the den. In good shape."

"Put them in the trunk and take a look around outside. There may be an additional storage place. Did you find a computer?"

"Yep. I'll look at it later. Sorted through some disks up there, but nothing like we're looking for."

"Okay, go ahead and stow the guns."

Boston nodded and left.

Marciano stared at Trish for a minute and then sat forward in his chair. "Shall we find something to eat? I'm famished."

Trish got up and headed to the kitchen. *Well, I'm not famished. I wonder if there is any rat poison in the cabinets?*

Chapter Thirty-Five

Marciano stood in the doorway, cleaning his fingernails with a jackknife. Trish rummaged through the kitchen cabinets trying to find something to throw on a plate for Namu.

Drat, no rat poison. Hmm, I wonder what Windex would do to Marciano's insides? Better not do that. He's liable to make me taste the food first.

The search yielded canned ham, peaches, and a jar of olives stuffed with jalapenos. She also found a jar of peanut butter and a sealed tin of crackers. "There. Help yourself. A feast fit for a dirt bag." She tossed them all on the kitchen table.

Marciano laughed, lifted the pull-tab, and removed the lid from the peaches. "You're not going to make me angry. Everything is going my way. All I have to do is find my financial records and I'll be out of here."

Trish eased toward the silverware drawer. *If I could get to that butcher knife, I could do a little carving of my own. If that doesn't work, there's always the storage safe in the den.*

Boston appeared and grabbed the peanut butter. He dipped two fingers inside the jar and began shoving chunky globs into his mouth.

Marciano suddenly knocked the jar from Boston's hand. It hit the front of the stainless steel refrigerator and fell to the floor, not losing a drop from inside.

"Have some manners, you oaf. Ask before you just assume this food is for you."

Boston stared at Marciano and smiled as he continued licking his fingers.

"Pick up the jar and place it on the table." Marciano gritted his teeth. "Please."

Boston retrieved the jar and banged it on the table. He placed his hands on the table and leaned down to his boss. "Good thing it's plastic. Otherwise you wouldn't have anything to put on your crackers."

Marciano's movement was so quick Trish almost couldn't follow it. The knife the big man had used to threaten her, stabbed into the wooden tabletop. It quivered between the thumb and forefinger of Boston's right hand. Marciano stood and stared at Boston. "If I didn't need both your hands in working condition, I'd have thrust that an inch to the right and you'd be howling like a newborn. Don't cross me, Boston. Ever!"

Boston looked at Marciano and down at his hand. "Nice move, boss." He smiled and with extra effort pulled out the knife and handed it back to Marciano.

Trish realized the worst thing about the altercation was she'd been paralyzed and hadn't taken the opportunity to grab the butcher knife. She mentally kicked herself.

"Be a good boy, Boston, and find a place we can stow Mrs. Morgan while we do our search."

"There's a den down the hall. No windows and a nice healthy lock on the outside of the door."

Marciano nodded and returned to his meal.

Trish breathed a sigh of relief. First, because she would have had to clean up the blood if any had been spilled. Second, because Boston had not found the trap door in the den. Jim had shown her where it was and what was inside. He'd forced her to spend hours at target practice with several weapons. She hoped the pistol was still there. And she prayed she would be able to go through with her plan. She didn't like shooting animals, and she darn well knew she didn't want to shoot a human.

I seem to have no choice. And these dolts are more like animals anyway. Can I really do it? Shooting Davis was an accident. This is different.

Boston took her arm and pushed her toward the hallway. "Let's go, lady. We have work to do."

Trish wriggled her arm away and headed to the den.

Once inside she was shoved onto a couch, Boston pulled out another of the ever-present plastic wires for her wrists. He did the same to her feet.

Damn, I didn't think about being tied up again. "Hey, I don't need any plastic bracelets. I'm not going anywhere."

"Merely a precaution. Don't like taking chances. Even with a woman."

You wait, buster. You'll think just a woman.

He turned around and unplugged the computer tower. Two trips cleared the desk of terminal and tower. He gave Trish a little wave before he closed and locked the door.

I need to get out of these shackles. The hardwood floors converted small noises to giant ones, so she removed her shoes, got up, and hobbled over to the door. Placing her ear against the surface, she listened to the voices in the kitchen.

Good, they're both in there. She hopped over to the desk. The drawers yielded nothing useful. Then she spotted what she needed. Resting in the pencil holder was a letter opener commemorating their credit union's 35th anniversary.

Trish held the tool between her middle finger and her palm to push the strip through. It took a couple of minutes of sawing, but it worked. She snipped the thin plastic wire from her wrists and then her feet. She stepped to the door again and listened. Muted voices still emanated from the kitchen.

She crept to the desk. *I sure hope some weapons are here.* Trish grabbed the front of the desk and pulled slowly. *Thank God, Jim put rubber wheels on this thing.* The desk moved. Carefully, she tugged it to the center of the room. Underneath the desk an oriental rug covered the trap door. It was more like a safe in the floor complete with a combination lock.

Crap. What was the combination? Think, Trish, think. She tried Jim's birthday, her birthday, and his mother's birthday. Nothing. *I know it was a date. But what date? Wait a minute. I don't suppose he'd use that, would he?* She turned the tumblers. Three, seventeen, ninety-eight. A satisfying click sounded as she turned to the last number. *Our wedding date. Who'd have thought?*

The lid creaked as she opened it. Trish cringed. *No time to worry about that now. What's in here?* Her heart sank. No gun. All those hours of practice, and Jim didn't even keep a pistol. *Damn it, Jim. Couldn't you do this right? All that talk about my safety and how this would be our fallback if something was to happen. All you left was a bow and arrows?*

She got up and checked at the door again, listening for any indication her captors would come make sure she was still tied up. Only distant footsteps on the wood floor in the kitchen. She took a shuddering breath and returned to the safe. Trish knelt down and pulled out the case. Inside was her Mathews bow. *This'll have to do.*

Chapter Thirty-Six

"You'll see. This will be fun. You and me out in the woods. The thrill of the hunt."

That had been three years ago when Jim set up the target and scurried around unpacking the equipment. Then two new metal carrying cases lay open in the grass behind the cabin. A his-and-hers set of Mathews bows sparkled in the sunlight. A Switchback for Jim and a Mustang for Trish.

She shivered in spite of the warm summer breeze. She pushed back strands of blowing hair and stared as Jim assembled the bow. Her bow. She barely heard the instructions at first. Talk of a perimeter-weighted cam, Harmonic dampers, string suppressors, and roller guard was all Greek to her. No amount of pleading, crying, or resistance had swayed Jim from forcing her to be here.

"Jim, I really don't understand this. I will not shoot a defenseless deer."

Jim laughed. "Honey, think of it like this. We are helping control the deer population. They need to be thinned so they won't starve in the winter." He continued setting up. "You don't want that, do you?"

Crap. He's actually whistling.

Too soon she was in a stance in front of the target. "Pull steady." He told her. "Ease back the arrow. Take a breath and release."

Her arms were on fire. She couldn't hold any

longer. The strain was so great she felt as if her shoulder would pop out of its socket. Her right arm began to shake, and she had to let go. The arrow shot up in the air and landed in the river.

Jim shook his head. He slowly walked to the target and moved it so it was not facing the river. With giant steps, he paced off the distance back to her and smiled. "We can't afford to lose arrows. They aren't cheap, you know. Now let's try again."

They had spent hours practicing. Trish's shoulders hurt so much she couldn't lift a skillet to cook supper that night. Since that time, Trish had become a very good archer. She could hit a bull's-eye three out of five times from over one hundred yards.

The dreaded day came when Jim said she was ready for the hunt. Again, she told him she could not do it. She couldn't hurt a wild animal. But she also didn't dare do anything but follow Jim's commands.

He had smiled and said, "Once you're out there and see the deer you'll be fine. It's the only way to get venison steaks. Wait till you taste one of those. Oh wow. Just like the hunters of old, bagging game and feasting on the spoils."

A three-hour wait secured to a tree had her close to tears. She needed to go to the bathroom. Jim told her to shut up. He whispered and it drove her nuts. Then a deer came stepping slowly toward their position. Jim nudged her. She pulled back on the bow as he'd preached. The deer came to a perfect position. She zeroed down the sight and those big, sorrowful eyes peered directly into her brain. Its ear twitched. She still didn't know why but she let the arrow fly. Time stood still. She was almost riding on top of the arrow as it thudded into the unsuspecting beast. It staggered, turned, and leaped over a clump of brush. All she saw was that wisp of tail bounding off into the trees.

"Oh, what a great shot, Trish. A bulls-eye. Keep an eye on her. Watch where she goes." He hugged her. While her teeth chattered, she used his strength to remain standing. She stood stiff and sick, and trembled inwardly.

They waited for about ten minutes, then climbed down from their perch. As soon as Trish hit the ground, she threw up. Her stomach was roiling and she doubled over to ease the pain. Jim was oblivious. He was so enthralled with the kill he almost left Trish to get the deer.

He grabbed her arm. "Come on, we've got to find your trophy."

She wriggled away. "I can't. You go on. I'm sick."

"You can't miss the best part. Finding the quarry and bringing it home. Come on." He trudged off into the brush.

Trish didn't know how she made it through that day. The deer was 250 yards from where she murdered it. The trail of blood was easy to spot. When they reached the dead animal, Trish averted her eyes from its face. The arrow protruded from its side and a trail of blood ran from the wound. Trish's stomach was empty and she suffered through a session of dry heaves.

Then she made the mistake of looking at the head. Dead eyes wide in fright stared at her, convicting her and leaving an image that haunted her.

She wanted to die in that poor animal's place. That moment was when she began to hate Jim.

Chapter Thirty-Seven

Trish took the case from the safe and wasted no time assembling the bow. Her life was on the line. She flexed the bow to regain the muscle memory from hours of practice. Her shoulders strained from inactivity with the bow. But, somehow it felt good. She was not completely at the mercy of Marciano and Boston. She could fight back.

Trish listened at the door again to determine her adversaries' location. Still in the kitchen. She formed a plan, to make her stand in the corner of the room.

Four metal tipped arrows lay in the bow case. She brought them out wondering again if she had the guts to release an arrow toward a living being. *I have to. Lord, give me strength.*

An easy chair occupied the corner opposite the door, beside it was a small table containing a lamp. Trish laid the arrows on the table and moved the chair to one side. She stood in the corner and aimed her bow at the door to judge the distance. Best to keep the light off. That way the arrow would be coming from the darkest part of the den to add to the element of surprise. *I guess all I can do now is wait for them to make a move.*

A million thoughts roamed through her mind. *What if both men come in? What if I can't shoot? What if Marciano comes in? He's so big an arrow won't stop him. For that matter, I don't know if an arrow would stop Boston.* She remembered Jim saying a 200-pound deer would take an arrow and run for a long distance. How would it affect a 200-plus-pound man? Why hadn't Jim left at least one gun in the safe? *Oh, God, just let me get out of this alive. Please.*

Trish went to the door and pressed her ear to the cold wood. She could make out some conversation.

"What about this file here, boss?"

"Looks promising. Bring it up." Long pause. "That's the big one. These others must be the various accounts. Very good, Boston. Copy them onto the flash drive and let's get out of here."

"What about the woman?"

"You know what to do. When you get the files copied, I'll take them out to the car. You clean up the rest of this mess. After you do that, there must be something around here you can use to start a nice fire."

"Yeah. There's some stuff in the kitchen. No problem."

Trish caught her breath. A fire? She looked at the log walls. The place would go up in minutes. She strained to hear more.

They continued to copy files and make plans to get away.

Finally, Marciano said, "Good, we're done. I'll wait in the car. You finish up."

"Right."

Trish forced air into her lungs. *This is it. Just wish I could make my hands stop shaking.* The front door slammed a few seconds later. Boston began rummaging in the kitchen cabinets. Trish hurried to the corner and grabbed her bow. She fixed an arrow against the string and waited.

An eternity passed until the lock to the den door wiggled. She aimed the bow at the middle of the door and pulled back as far as she could. The door opened. Boston filled the space.

"What the hell?" His eyes opened wide.

Trish concentrated. She had heard that in times like this things happen in slow motion. Whoever said that was right. Sweat trickled down her back. She stretched to her full height. *Exhale. Steady. Release.* The arrow flew to its target. It seemed to take a long time to reach Boston. The sound of the arrow hitting flesh was followed by a solid thunk as the tip passed through the man and into the door, leaving the feathers protruding from his chest.

"Ummm. No." Boston looked down at the shaft. He tried to move. He looked up at Trish and his eyes darkened.

Trish readied another arrow and aimed.

The wounded man yanked at the shaft, but could not pull it out. He looked behind him, and with great effort, jerked his body away from the door. The arrow was still stuck in the wood. Boston lunged toward Trish. She released a second arrow. This one caught him between the ribs.

Boston kept coming. Bloody hands reached out. They grabbed Trish in a bear hug. He still had a tremendous amount of strength left.

She tried to brace her legs but his weight was too much for her. They dropped to the floor. His breath was bad. He rolled on top of her; all the air rushed out of her lungs. She couldn't breathe.

Kicking, scratching, and biting Boston only made

him squeeze harder. Her hands were pinned to her side. Sticky, warm liquid gushed over her right arm. *God, it's his blood.* She lost consciousness as Boston groaned once more.

Chapter Thirty-Eight

When Trish regained consciousness Boston was still on top of her. *Lord, a Hummer would be lighter.* She heaved him off to one side with a shove that cost all of her remaining strength. Inhaling was difficult but she finally got enough air to fill her lungs.

Was he dead? With effort, Trish sat up and crawled over to him, careful to avoid the pool of blood around his side. No pulse. Funny, she didn't have the same reaction with Boston as she'd had with the deer. *Maybe because the deer deserved to live.*

She scrambled to her feet and peeked out the door of the den. Marciano was nowhere in sight. She prayed he was still outside in the car. Willing her stomach to calm down, Trish stood over Boston and searched his pockets. A pistol, two knives, and a small leather case full of odd-looking tools were piled beside the man.

The pistol was a Smith & Wesson. An unfamiliar brand. The only pistol Jim had shown her how to shoot was his Glock 22. *How does this thing work? Crap, it seems heavy enough but I can't even tell if it's loaded.* She tried to figure it out while being careful not to shoot herself. She flipped off the safety, though without firing the weapon she couldn't be sure it would do her any good.

The back door banged shut.

"What the hell's taking you so long? We need to

get out of here."

Oh no, he's back. Trish dropped the gun on the desk and grabbed her bow and an arrow. Marciano appeared at the door.

"What the…" He grabbed the doorframe his eyes focused on the arrow pointed at his chest.

Trish put what she hoped was a menacing gaze on her face. "Don't move or Boston won't be the only one leaking on the floor."

Marciano gave her a half-hearted smile and glanced at the inert form of his former bodyguard. "Seems you have me at a disadvantage. What now? Are you going to shoot me?"

"If you force me to, I will. I'm an excellent shot."

"I can see that. I'm, um…leaving. I have everything I need." He pulled the door shut and Trish heard the lock being turned.

Shit! Well, let him go. Let the cops take care of him. I've got to figure out how to get out of here. Then she heard Marciano stirring in the next room. She moved to the door and listened. He was opening drawers and cabinets looking for something. *What the heck is he doing? I thought he was leaving.*

The movement stopped. She didn't hear the front door open and close. *Why doesn't he just leave?* For two or three minutes, she heard nothing. Then splashing in the hallway. Whoosh. Almost immediately, she smelled smoke. *The SOB is setting the place on fire.*

The front door opened and slammed shut.

Even though she knew the den door was locked, Trish tried the knob. No movement. Damn. She hurried back to the desk for the gun. She took aim at the lock and fired. Splinters flew from the impact. Three more times bullets thudded into the door. Trish tried the knob again and felt some give. *Come on. You've got to open.* Smoke began seeping under the door.

Trish put three more shots into the frame around the latch. She tried the door again. The knob refused to turn at all. Frustrated, she kicked the knob. It broke free. She rushed into the hall. Smoke burned her eyes and filled her nose. She dropped to the floor. Flames licked at her from both sides of the hall. With her free hand, she tugged her blouse up over her face, breathing through the fabric. Awkwardly, with one hand as a balance, she crawled down the hall, pushing the pistol in front of her. The heat was unbearable; it singed the fine hairs on her arms.

When she reached the front door her heart sank. Through the window, she saw Marciano squatting in front of a pile of wood blocking her from the door. He looked up at Trish as flames escaped from the pile. A grin spread across his face.

Trish picked up the Smith & Wesson and aimed it at that face. The grin disappeared. So did Marciano. He scrambled down the porch steps and headed toward his car.

The fire was just behind Trish. Heat crawled up her back. She prayed her clothes were not in flames. She had to get outside. Grabbing the barrel of the gun, she pounded on the window next to the door. It took four blows before the window broke.

Marciano threw open the car door and jumped inside. Trish took aim and fired. She managed to hit the three tires she could see. Marciano looked back at her and revved up the Mercedes. Gravel flew from the front tires; the car lurched forward. Trish aimed at the driver and squeezed the trigger again. The gun clicked but nothing happened. *Damn, out of bullets.*

She could only watch as the Mercedes swerved down the road. Suddenly, the car skidded to a stop. Three police cars, lights flashing, blocked the road. Marciano threw open the door and pounded the top of the car. He raised his hands and glared back at Trish.

Finally, the window frame was clear of glass for her to climb out. Two officers rushed to help and lifted her out of the window. Mumbling what she hoped would be understood as thanks, Trish collapsed on the bank of the river several yards from the cabin. With a loud crack, the cabin disintegrated in flames. She rubbed soothing water on her arms and washed her face. And thanked God she was alive.

Chapter Thirty-Nine

The firemen were fighting a losing battle. Police and FBI agents gathered and marked evidence. One of the officers had given Trish a blanket, which did not keep her from shivering. Exhaustion was taking over. She had answered questions and given statements for the last hour. She had hoped to be driven home by now but that didn't look promising any time soon.

Agent Cheever rocked back on his heels and cleared his throat. "Well, Mrs. Morgan, you've had quite an experience."

"Cheever, you always seem to be able to sum things up, albeit after the fact. Do you think you might persuade someone to drive me home? I'm going to jump into a nice relaxing bath and get some sleep."

Cheever looked around and shrugged. "Not right now. We have a few things to finish up. I don't have any agents to spare right now."

Bob Jenkins appeared at Cheever's side. "Don't fret yourself, old man. I'm taking the lady home right now. You have no objection, do you?"

Trish was never so glad to see anyone in her life. "Bob, how did you know?"

"I ferried one of Cheever's agents up here just now. I'm ready to go back." Jenkins reached down and helped Trish to her feet.

Cheever looked perplexed. "Um, I guess that's

okay. Where will you be in case we need you?"

"At the bed and breakfast." Trish gave him a steely stare. "But you won't need me tonight. I'll be resting."

They walked to Bob's squad car.

"That was so nice of you, Officer."

"Officer? What happened to just Bob?"

Trish smiled. "Well, I guess under the circumstances, Bob would be okay."

Trish stumbled. Bob reached out and caught her. "Steady there. Hold my arm. Don't want our star witness to get hurt after all she's been through."

"Thanks, Bob." His arm surrounded her with warmth and strength. She finally felt comfortable.

****

The long, ride back was filled with conversation. Trish opened up to Bob more than she ever had intended. He seemed interested in everything she said. She was tired, but buoyed by the release of tension she enjoyed having a conversation with someone who treated her with respect. That had been a rare happening in her married life. It was refreshing.

"Now that this part of your life is over, what are your plans?" Bob's eyes seldom left the road, but now he searched her face.

"I'm not sure. I've got some ideas, but they're sketchy. A lot of things depend on finding out if I passed my bar exam."

"Oh, I'm sure you passed. You're smart. There's no way you failed. I know it."

"Thanks for the vote of confidence. I wish I was that sure."

"Would it be okay if I took you to dinner some night? I enjoy talking to you."

Trish leaned back in her seat. She studied Bob and then nodded. "I'd like that."

They didn't run out of things to talk about all the way to the bed and breakfast. Bob walked her to the door and helped her with the key.

"Good night, Bob. Thanks again for the ride. And for everything."

"You're more than welcome. Good night, Trish." She turned to go in and Bob gently touched her shoulders. "I'm so glad you were able to get away. I was worried. There was nothing I could do. If something had happened, I'd never have forgiven myself."

"You couldn't do anything. I was lucky—that's all."

"All right, if that's the way you feel. Anyway, to see you huddled in that blanket, scared and maybe injured, just made my heart break. I'm glad you're here and well, I'm real happy." Then he kissed her on the forehead and went down the steps two at a time.

He sped off and Trish looked at the kitchen window. Bev's face was plastered against the pane. She smiled and winked.

Trish blushed and hurried inside. She could still feel Bob's lips touching her forehead. It felt right.

Epilogue

Jim's funeral was both somber and surreal. Rain poured off the umbrella borrowed from the funeral home. Trish stood among a small crowd, ruing wearing heels and regretting the curtness to her mother-in-law. Jim's mother had openly blamed Trish for this whole mess, but it did not excuse Trish's retort. She had lost her cool.

This does nothing to quell my hatred of funerals. They're bad enough, but when it rains, they're miserable. Why didn't she feel sad? She had loved Jim, at least at first.

The funeral was somber because of Jim's murder but surreal since Trish could not rid her mind that the unhappy days had far outnumbered the happy ones. Thankfully, the verbal abuse and ugliness of her life was in the past. It also marked the beginning of her new life. And, she thought with pride, lawyer could now be fixed onto her résumé. She had received the letter that same day affirming she'd passed the bar exam.

Other than Jim's mom, the family tolerated her. She was relieved when they opted to ride in a separate car. Only Jim's younger brother Ron seemed genuine in his sympathy. He gave her hand a squeeze and told her to call him anytime. Early in their marriage, the two brothers had often reminisced by exchanging hilarious childhood stories. Those were the days when the marriage had been strong. What a sad turn of events when Jim's dad died and Jim had begun to work for that company. His personality changed, and he had become someone Trish didn't know. At times more like someone she didn't want to know.

The entire staff of Spitzer, Walters, Walters, & Sloan made an appearance, except for the late Mr. Spitzer. Walters and Walters bumped into each other trying to be at the head of the firm's procession. A mutual cease-fire took place as they settled for side-by-side. Charity latched onto one of the pallbearers and chatted away like they were old friends. They probably would be soon.

When Trish submitted her resignation, Mr. Sloan had been surprisingly speechless. Then, uncharacteristically, he patted her shoulder and wished her the best. He mumbled something about being sad to see her go and left fumbling for his handkerchief, a touching moment that meant a lot to her.

Trish wandered back to the hearse through the oak trees, trying to ignore the rainwater sliding down her back. Her life was in a state of flux. Between jobs, preparing for a move, regretting leaving her best friend, and yet tasting the excitement of new opportunities and challenges. She was free from the stress of the last two years.

Heather fell into step with Trish trying to avoid treading on any plot markers. "I'm so sorry things with you and Jim didn't work out but, I've got to tell you, you deserve better. Gonna be hell to work in that place without you. Why couldn't you find a job in Chicago?"

"Wasn't in the cards. I'm going to miss you, too. Listen, I don't want you to shoot anyone after I leave."

Heather grinned. "Only if they deserve it. Wow, that could be a lot of people. Guess I better watch myself. And you watch yourself, too, you hear? Keep in touch and look out. You never know when I might just bop over to D. C. and invite myself to stay with you."

"That's a deal. I'd love it." They embraced and Trish heard Heather sniffle. "Look, I still have a week before I leave to find a place to live. Let's do it up right. Give me a call tomorrow."

"You got it. Look out, Chicago." Heather, with a bright-pink umbrella held high, walked up to Max and slipped her arm into his. She looked back at Trish and winked. "Hey, I just thought, if we get into trouble you can represent us."

Trish yelled back, "It'll be on the house."

When she arrived at the hearse, Bev stood next to the limo dabbing her eyes. She blew into the handkerchief. "You know everything works out in God's plan. I think He has great things in store for you. Just follow your heart and you'll be fine. Remember, I'm just a phone call away if you ever need anyone to talk to."

Trish squeezed Bev's hand. "I truly appreciate that. I'm going to miss you."

"Shucks, don't make me cry anymore. Oh, Bob was looking for you a while ago. Did he find you?"

"He did. He wanted to tell me they found out what Marciano was after. Those files were his Cayman Island bank records. Almost five hundred million deposited in hundreds of accounts. Jim had encoded the numbers but the FBI broke the code and will recover the money."

"Good news for sure."

"Yes, really. They said the code was a simple one and amateurishly done. They believe Jim did it that way on purpose so the money wouldn't be lost. Makes me feel a little better. Jim wasn't a saint by any means but he had a spark of something good in him. That's what I saw when we first met."

"Don't you forget, you're a good judge of character." Bev's bright-blue eyes twinkled; a smile softened her wrinkled face. "Take Bob for instance."

Trish laughed. "I get the picture, Bev. Looks like Bob and I will be working within minutes of each other. I'm interning at a firm in Washington."

"How marvelous. I hadn't heard where you would be. Bob's going to be very pleased."

"I just found out about it this morning. Had my application in for almost six months."

"What'd I tell you about a plan?" Bev nudged Trish with an elbow. "Bob's a great person. Give him a chance." Bev walked slowly down the rock path.

Yes, Bob is a good person. Maybe I will give him a chance.

"You're smiling. Are you thinking about me?" Bob appeared beside her and opened the limousine door.

Trish knew her neck and face were flushing the color of cinnamon candy. "Just thinking about the next chapter of my life."

"What do you have planned?"

"A new job at a Washington law firm."

He smiled. "Washington D. C.?"

"Yes, D.C."

"I hope you'll find time for an old friend."

She grinned and climbed inside. "You're not so old."

Bob leaned in and said, "Careful, counselor. I might take that as encouragement."

Counselor. That sounds wonderful.

Maybe it was a hint. Maybe it was more than a hint. After all, secrets, deception, and greed were in the past. Thank God.

The future didn't have a single smudge on it.

A word about the author...

I have always written, mostly short stories until I "retired" in 2002. Then I had mysteries in trade paperback and eBook published.

I'm active in over twenty yahoo groups about writing, and I own and moderate the Publishing and Promoting group with over 1000 authors and publishers worldwide providing a free source of tips and information pertaining to writing.

I will be teaching an online three-week course titled How to Add Suspense to Your Killer Novel for Savvy Authors in 2014. This is a repeat course that I did in 2010.

Visit me on http://jdwebb.com